## The leopard froze in midstride and sniffed again—man smell!

Bolan's every sense was alert...and some survival instinct far below his consciousness compelled him to turn. Alarms were screaming in his brain as he whirled.

One hundred twenty pounds of hunger-maddened savagery, taut muscle and slashing fangs smashed into him. Bolan's weapon was knocked from his hand.

With a lightning-fast maneuver, The Executioner straddled the great cat. It writhed and twisted, snarling, desperate to shake off Bolan's weight, but his grip tightened. Each agonizing second lasted an eternity.

Then the creature found new reserves of strength and began to squirm out from under him....

Also available from Gold Eagle Books,
publishers of the Executioner series:

Mack Bolan's
# ABLE TEAM

#1 Tower of Terror
#2 The Hostaged Island
#3 Texas Showdown
#4 Amazon Slaughter
#5 Cairo Countdown
#6 Warlord of Azatlan
#7 Justice by Fire
#8 Army of Devils

Mack Bolan's
# PHOENIX FORCE

#1 Argentine Deadline
#2 Guerilla Games
#3 Atlantic Scramble
#4 Tigers of Justice
#5 The Fury Bombs
#6 White Hell
#7 Dragon's Kill

# MACK BOLAN

THE EXECUTIONER 58

## BOLAN

**Ambush on Blood River**

A GOLD EAGLE BOOK FROM

# WORLDWIDE

TORONTO · NEW YORK · LONDON · PARIS
AMSTERDAM · STOCKHOLM · HAMBURG
ATHENS · MILAN · TOKYO · SYDNEY

First edition October 1983

ISBN 0-373-61058-0

Special thanks and acknowledgment to
Alan Bomack for his contributions to this work.

Printed in Canada

# 1

Mack Bolan shifted the gun to his left hand. It did not matter. He was just as accurate with either.

It was a much lighter piece than he was used to; but that, too, made no difference.

Bending slightly forward, the big man gently pushed aside the thin foliage with his right hand. His suggestion of a smile showed white even teeth, and this expression of almost boyish concentration was the only thing that softened the hard glint of satisfaction in his fierce blue eyes.

They were to his right, and slightly below him. Three soldiers.

Two of them, both wearing camouflage jackets bought in the same army-surplus store in downtown Toronto, were lying behind a fallen log. The crisp, bold designs of sandy brown, black and olive stood out against the thin powdery trace of last night's brief snowfall. The third guy, only his face peering out of his parka hood, was crouching behind a moss-speckled rock.

A yellow flag, the pennant they were guarding, hung from the lowest branch of a nearby maple. The three were the last remaining survivors of Yellow Team.

There had been seven of them at the start. And they had grumbled when Jeff Clayton, who ran the Survivalcraft Game, introduced them to the Blue Team: John Phoenix, who had just flown up from the States, and Gary Manning, who had come down from Montreal.

Only two men against seven!

Keith Duffin, a bald accountant from Downsview, a Toronto suburb, had muttered under his breath that he'd ask for his money back if Clayton was going to make it this easy. And Glen Grant, who had been "killed" on both his previous visits, sniggered at the prospect of scoring for himself at last. He especially wanted to get the tall American; standing in the car park, the man's cool assurance had irritated him.

Blue Team's flag was right where they had left it, dangling from the bare twigs of a birch tree half a mile behind them. Four of the Yellow Team had "died" trying to reach it. Duffin and Grant were right. The game was much too one-sided, but in Blue Team's favor.

Gary Manning referred to Bolan only by his new identity as Colonel John Phoenix, the founding force of Phoenix Force, his crack squad of international warriors; and Manning had been advised not to use Bolan's rank.

The Canadian had waited for Phoenix to signal left or right.

"Gary, take the right flank," Bolan had suggested.

The two men separated, crept swiftly through the

bush, and took up their respective positions to cover any approach to the Blue Team's flag.

Manning made the first hit. He wiped the sneer off Duffin's flabby face when his shot smeared the accountant's bald top with a streak of blue paint.

A few minutes later Bolan let Grant squirm right past him. He waited till the supermarket manager was feeling secure behind a small fir tree before hissing, "Grant!"

The other man turned and found himself staring down the business end of a Nel-Spot $CO_2$ marker gun. Bolan squeezed the trigger.

The .68-caliber gelatin ball struck the front of Grant's jacket right over the heart and splattered him with a bright blue stain.

Bolan hit two more of the Yellow Team players as they moved forward warily toward the rival flag. "Just a goddamned game," he muttered impatiently to himself. The object of it was to seize the other team's pennant and deliver it to the shack at the top of the ridge without being marked by a splash from a Nel-Spot.

Now Bolan and Manning were poised within two hundred yards of their goal. Bolan slowly set the skinny branches back into place. He glanced over to his right. His companion blended perfectly with the frost-rimmed foliage.

Manning's bush jacket had started out plain drab, but it had acquired its own camouflage over the years—grass burns, mud, blood and stains from half a dozen actions. All Bolan could see was his blue armband; even Manning's face had disappeared behind a mask of tricolor combat cosmetics.

Bolan jabbed his finger downslope toward the opposition, then held up three fingers to Manning.

Manning nodded. He understood.

Bolan silently indicated he would work his way farther along the side of the slope. Neither man had to consult the topographic maps they'd been given: both had quickly memorized the salient features of the terrain. Manning knew that Phoenix was going to try for the solitary tree at the end of the bare spur directly overlooking Yellow Team's base. Manning also knew the part he would have to play in achieving that objective.

He adjusted his protective goggles and waited for Phoenix to get into position.

Bolan squatted behind the last low bush. There were only fifteen yards of snow-dusted grass tussocks between him and the tree.

Bolan picked up a length of rotted wood and tossed it back the way he had come. It drew a round of fire from the enemy.

Manning made his move. He fired once to divert attention, then rolled across the bare patch of ground toward a large pink-veined boulder. This time the two guys behind the log stood up to aim at their slithering, elusive target.

They missed.

And Bolan gained the tree.

"Up there!" The fellow behind the rock pointed toward Bolan's superior position. He only showed his hand for a moment. But it was enough for Gary

Manning to hit it with a speeding blue paint ball.

Two to go.

Both of the enemy fired at the tree above them, marking it with bright splotches of yellow.

Manning jumped out from behind his cover with a blood-curdling war cry. The two amateurs whirled to face this unexpected threat. Which was when Bolan stepped into the open and ''killed'' them both instantly.

Blue Team had played no tricky or fancy games. Phoenix and Manning were not the sort to show off what they were really capable of—it had just been the systematic elimination of seven opponents in a war game.

Manning strolled forward, swung himself over the tree trunk and collected the yellow flag.

He clambered up the gravel-faced slope to where Colonel Phoenix was waiting for him.

Bolan glanced at the shack behind them. A flash of light caught his attention. Clayton must have had a clear view of the finish through his binoculars. ''Think we passed the test?''

''I'd say so, Colonel.'' The others were out of earshot as Manning handed him the pennant. ''Yes, I think we've passed with flying colors.''

''How LONG have you known this guy?'' Bolan asked, as they drove back into town.

''Jeff Clayton? About seven or eight years,'' replied Manning. ''Ever since he opened the CP. I usually stop by there when I'm in Toronto.''

''The CP?''

"It's the name of the bar he opened," explained the Canadian, shifting gears smoothly as the Ferrari powered up the hill.

The Ferrari 308GTS was the one indulgence Gary Manning allowed himself; apart from this magnificent machine, he lived a very Spartan life-style. It was the way he preferred it, everything else stripped down to bare essentials.

Suddenly an insistent flashing from a red LED warning light appeared on the Ferrari's dashboard. "Uh-oh, radar trap ahead."

Manning geared down and eased into the driving lane, cruising just below the limit. It gave him time to fill in Colonel Phoenix with more details.

"Jeff Clayton was a Green Beret. One of the best. But he returned to a country that didn't seem to give a damn for men like him or, worse, for the sacrifice made by the buddies he'd left behind. He drifted around the world as a merc for a while, then met and married a Canadian woman. Settled down in Toronto and opened the CP. It's a bar, well, more like a private club, that attracts a clientele of ex-servicemen, mercenaries, wildcatters, hunters and would-be adventurers. This Survivalcraft Game is his latest scheme."

"Of course the bar is an ideal place to recruit weekend soldiers?"

"Right. It's also a place they can come back to and shoot the breeze about their heroics."

"And this is where you heard about the African deal?"

Manning drove almost primly past the unmarked

police cruiser. Bolan lit a cigarette and waited for the cool Canadian to continue.

"Yeah. I'd come down to Toronto to pick up some electronic parts for a new version of the briefcase scrambler. Figured a way to make it even more effective. It's now fully compatible with the Stony Man net. It means we can place a call from a phone anywhere in the world and maintain full security."

"It sounds useful. I'd like to see it."

"Anyway, I stopped by the CP for a quick beer and Clayton mentioned this job to me. No details. . . but enough to get me interested."

"Like the money, for instance."

"That's what made me suspicious, yes," confirmed Manning. "It also made me think you might be interested in hearing about it."

"Fifty thousand dollars apiece?"

"It's what Clayton said: fifty thou each. Five men. For five or six days' work." Manning shook his head and glanced across at Bolan. "It's way above the market rates. Something big's going down."

The Canadian checked the side mirror as he swung off the cloverleaf and slipped into the steady stream of traffic on the divided highway.

Bolan pondered the implications of such a sizable fee. "If the pay's so good, how come Clayton doesn't put together a team himself?"

"Why should he? He's making quite enough money from the bar and the survivalist games to keep himself comfortable without risking life or limb."

Bolan was silent for a moment. He did not wage his own war for profit but for far more personal reasons. Still, it seemed to make sense. "And he hasn't mentioned this operation to anyone else?"

"Not as far as I know. When I walked into the CP, Clayton said he was about to give me a call. Claimed I was the only one he knew who might be up to it. I hinted that I had some friends who might like a slice of the action."

"So he suggested you invite them out to his weekend war games?" Bolan finished simply.

"Yeah, because he wanted to look us over before giving out any more info. I couldn't get hold of Katz, he was on his way to Paris."

"Israel's other front," grunted the big American. He knew Yakov Katzenelenbogen was in Paris to investigate another round of bomb threats against French Jews. Katz had a personal interest in that particular battleground—his wife had been killed in a car "accident" there.

"I think we acquitted ourselves well this afternoon," said Manning. "By the time we get to the CP, Clayton should be back there."

"Well, we'll have to put him in the mood to talk."

It was dark and the temperature was dropping fast by the time Bolan and Manning drove across town to visit Jeff Clayton's bar.

Manning circled the block looking for an empty parking space, gave up the search and double-parked in the reserved area outside a minor government office.

"It's less than a minute's walk," he said, adding nonchalantly, "I could do with a few days in the sun."

Bolan took a deep breath. It was cold enough to cause a prickling in the nostrils. He nodded in agreement.

South of the border it was coming up to Thanksgiving; here in Canada the post-harvesting Thanksgiving Day had already been celebrated six weeks earlier. They walked briskly, collars turned up against the biting cold.

There was nothing flashy on the outside to attract attention to the CP. In fact, Bolan would probably have walked right past it if Manning hadn't indicated the narrow doorway.

Inside, the long dark counter was scarred but well-polished.

Bolan glanced about him. Yes, the CP was cleverly designed and probably highly profitable. It was authentic enough to generate some real atmosphere.

It was unmistakably a man's bar. There were no videogames. And no pianist tinkling aimlessly in the corner. There were a dozen or so other guys already there. They all seemed right at home.

Manning strolled up to the bar to order two bottles of beer. Bolan inspected the green notice board: skydiving equipment for sale, and a brochure from Clayton to pull in more recruits for his weekend war games.

George, the bartender, slid the beer across to Gary. He carried them over to the table in the corner where Bolan was seated.

"Jeff's taking a call in the office," Manning explained. "He should be out in a minute. George has told him we're here."

A bellow of derisive laughter from a booth in the far corner made Bolan look across. "Isn't that the guy I hit between the shoulder blades today?"

"Yeah," said Manning, glancing over at the noisy group. "Jack Bruce, isn't it? Seems to be a real blowhard."

Bruce swung around just at the moment the newcomers were casually staring in his direction. He recognized them instantly. In fact, they were two men he would not forget in a hurry. He had taken an instant dislike to them the minute he'd seen them in that sleek Ferrari. And the American bastard was the one who had shot him in the back!

Bruce slid his legs out from under the booth table and swaggered over to the visitors.

Feet spread apart, Bruce stood next to Manning's shoulder. "You two think you got any right to be here?"

Before either man could reply, a pair of beefy arms gripped Bruce's torso from behind.

"They claimed their right this afternoon," said Jeff Clayton. His hold was light enough but clearly it could turn into a crushing bear hug at any second. Clayton obviously disliked sore losers. Bruce shrugged but it did nothing to loosen Clayton's grip on him.

Clayton turned Bruce about and steered him back toward his booth.

Clayton watched him for a few seconds before returning to the men who had come to see him. "Sorry about that. You always get a few rotten apples."

"It was just the drink talking." Bolan charitably dismissed the incident. "It's an interesting place you've got here."

"Thanks," Clayton acknowledged, pulling up another chair for himself. "You two did all right today. Yellow Team thought it was going to be a walkover. But you were the ones who made it look easy."

"It's a useful game," remarked Manning. "Keeps a guy's combat mind in gear."

"Gary tells me something else is happening around here. Another operation," probed Bolan. "And this time for real?"

Clayton raised both hands, palms outward. "It's not my operation. Let's get that straight up front. No, I was contacted to find out if I know any interested parties."

"We're an interested party."

"Ever been to Africa?" Clayton put the question to the American. Even when they had first been introduced in the car park at lunchtime, Clayton recognized John Phoenix as the man in command.

"North Africa," Bolan replied. "Never south of the Sahara."

Their host nodded. "It's a different world down there. Different rules. Hell, most of the time there aren't any rules."

Bolan understood that. His strategy was simple: an unending, unrelenting war against the forces of chaos, of senseless violence and intimidation, against terrorism in any form. But his tactics remained flexible. Providing the ethics were right and the call to duty clear and unavoidable, he could adapt his skills to any situation.

"What's the job?"

"I'm not completely sure," confessed Clayton. "And it's not up to me to tell you what little I do know. But I can give you a number. It's here in Ontario. You'll have to talk to Mr. Malakesi yourselves."

"Come on, Jeff, you already told me more than that. Is it Zaire?" guessed Manning. "Not Angola again?"

"How about in between? Right on the border

is my guess. Probably Kuranda. The old Congo has been subdivided into a whole new realm of political real estate. This thing goes back a long way.

"See Derek over there? The guy with the stubble. He was in the Congo in the sixties. With Five Commando. Mad Mike!" Clayton snorted at the wild stories he had been told of Major Mike Hoare and his mercenary brigade that quashed the Simba Revolt. He looked at Bolan again. "In this country we've got a leader who sings the praises of Andropov—the man who masterminded the KGB for years—and we vote him in as the prime minister. Over there, Mike Hoare tries to liberate an island from the grip of socialism gone mad and he ends up in jail. It's a topsy-turvy world, isn't it?"

Clayton saw agreement in those clear blue eyes. Without principles, without a just cause, Bolan thought, it was indeed a topsy-turvy world.

"Well, whoever's floating this mission has a bankroll behind them. There's a quarter of a million earmarked for the job. If you can do it with, say, five guys, that's fifty grand, for less than a week's work, I'm told."

"It sounds like a job for us. The money's right," said Bolan. But Clayton had no idea that this overly generous payment made no difference to the big American personally. In truth, it only aroused Bolan's suspicions. Mack Bolan was a soldier all right—but he fought for principles, not for pay.

Clayton made another guess of his own. "For my money, it's either a hit...or a treasure hunt."

He had their undivided attention.

"If it is in Kuranda, then the target would probably be General Mumungo. Maybe even the retarded boy-king himself, Buka Ntanga. Maybe it's both of them."

"And the treasure you mentioned?" asked Manning.

Clayton glanced around to make sure he couldn't be overheard. "Maybe at last someone's figured out where Scarr stashed his loot."

"Scarr?" Bolan was mentally filing the names. He would have April Rose run a check on them as soon as possible. Maybe Brognola in Washington could fill in more of the background.

"Brendan Scarr. A merc. From South Africa originally. He's doing time now in Angola. I guess fate caught up with him in the end."

"What was this about loot?" Manning persisted.

Bruce and his friends were leaving. Bruce looked at the three of them as he passed their table. His expression might have been a malevolent grin, but it seemed more like a sneer. No one said a word.

Clayton felt he had already told the newcomers more than he should; he took advantage of this interruption to ignore the question. Instead, he scribbled down the number. "Call this guy. He's the one who can tell you what this is all about. I've played my part."

Bolan got up and shook Clayton's hand. He looked the ex-Green Beret right in the eye. "Tell me one thing. If the money's so good, why don't you take a crack at it yourself?"

"Are you kidding?" Clayton smiled and spread his arms wide, his gesture encompassing the room as if to indicate that he was quite satisfied with what he had. "My old lady would kill me!"

A LIGHT SCATTERING of snowflakes was starting to drift down as they stepped out of the muggy warmth of Jeff Clayton's bar.

Manning felt awkward. Neither Colonel Phoenix himself nor any members of his tactical strike force were killers for hire. If this operation should prove to be nothing but a contract for an assassination, then Gary would have to apologize for bringing Bolan up here on a wild-goose chase.

But Bolan appeared to be interested. A quarter of a million dollars was a high price, even for a political hit. There would have been plenty of takers at a hundred thousand. No, there had to be more to it than that.

Bolan wanted to find out exactly what the score was with this Malakesi.

"If that scrambler unit of yours is on-line, we'll put it to work," he told Manning. "I'll get April Rose to run those names through Stony Man's computer—something's bound to show. Then we'll talk to this Malakesi character. Oh, yes, and I'd better find Katz."

"If you can."

"I think I know where he's staying in Paris. We'll have to contact everyone on the team and put them on standby. I've got a feeling we're going to have to move fast if...."

They had turned the corner and were almost on top of the Ferrari when they saw the three guys waiting for them.

A lanky dude in a Stetson and cowboy boots was propped against the hood. Jack Bruce stood by the door, a key ring bunched in his fist and a stupid grin on his face.

Even in the lurid yellow glow of the streetlights, they could see the long ugly gash that had been scraped deep in the Italian sports car's paintwork.

The third guy stopped smiling when Manning shook his head sadly and spoke. "I'm sorry you did that."

"Yeah?" sneered Bruce. "I just bet you are!"

Bolan stepped in front of the vandal and quietly corrected him. "No, he meant he was sorry for you."

The tense silence lasted only a few moments, but it might have been for much longer. Then The Executioner made his move. With three strides he was past the puzzled Bruce and closing quickly on the cowboy who was leaning against the damaged hood of the Ferrari.

As Bruce turned his head to follow the American's unexpected action, Gary Manning stepped in.

Jack Bruce tried to swivel around just as Manning drove a powerful right jab deep into the man's flabby beer gut. The spasm of pain that tore at his diaphragm bent Bruce forward, gasping for breath.

As Bruce doubled over, Manning's second shot was a left uppercut. Bruce's head snapped back, the column of his neck vulnerable to the onslaught of the burly Canadian whose hands, palms held together, now came slicing through the air like an ax blade at the man's exposed throat.

Jack Bruce spewed blood and beer on the slushy sidewalk.

Another searing paroxysm of pain tore at his vitals as Gary Manning's knee rammed into his crotch.

No petty satisfaction he might have gained from scratching the car could be worth the excruciating agony.

His body jackknifed forward again. Bruce could not even catch enough breath to scream. The hurting was totally bottled up inside and threatened to tear him apart.

His face connected with Manning's other knee, which was coming up with the force of a piston.

Bruce collapsed, whimpering, his nose smeared sideways across his face.

By the time Gary Manning had demolished Bruce, one of the other guys was crawling through the snow with a broken wrist and a split over his right eyebrow that was going to require several stitches to close. Bolan was chasing the cowboy down the street, close enough behind for one well-aimed kick to send the last of the crew sprawling in the gutter.

BOLAN WAS PLEASED. Today's action had shown how well Gary Manning worked with him. He had chosen the members of Phoenix Force well.

The Canadian was also smart and showed good initiative. The scrambler worked perfectly and was smaller than any they had used before.

Bolan held the receiver to his ear. The tone was

shorter, sharper than the customary North American one. At the other end, the phone was ringing in Paris.

Katz answered with a noncommittal, *"Oui, allô?"*

Bolan identified himself.

Katz listened attentively to the American's briefing.

"And so I've spoken to Malakesi. Gary and I have an appointment with him in the morning. The only thing he wanted to know was how quickly we were prepared to leave."

"Are you taking the whole team?"

"If I can get hold of them in time, yes."

"Do you need us all?"

"I'm not sure at this point. I don't know what the job is, but Clayton seemed to think it could be done by five men."

Katz weighed Bolan's reply before suggesting, "In that case, perhaps I should sit this one out."

For a moment Bolan wondered if Yakov Katzenelenbogen found the idea of being the CO a problem. Katz guessed he had provoked such a suspicion so he explained, "It's the Congo. I once said I would never go back. I'd like to be able to keep my word to myself."

"I understand," said Bolan, mentally reading between the lines of the short entry he remembered seeing in Katz's dossier. But he knew these men well. Bolan had brought them together. "Does the name Brendan Scarr mean anything to you?"

The second silence was even longer than the first. Then Katz asked crisply, "Where do we rendezvous?"

"If I give the go signal, we'll probably link up in Salisbury." Bolan did not correct himself and call the capital by its new name, Harare.

"Then I'll be there," Katz said. "You can count on it."

3

It was very late. Or very early in the morning. There was a morbid chill in the air and silver gray tendrils of mist snaked through the gardens and swirled along the Rue de Rivoli. Katz's mood now matched the weather. He was standing at the window, staring out over the silhouetted rooftops. The call from Colonel Phoenix left him brooding, unfocused and vaguely uneasy.

Katz thought he had said farewell to Africa.

He took a sip of cognac.

Damn the Congo!

And damn Scarr!

Katz took another sip and put down the glass.

He closed his eyes and rubbed his fingertips against the lids. He found himself absorbed by the swirling pattern of reds and gold and black. There was a word, a word in English, for that phenomenon.

Phos...phosphenes.

That's what they called the dizzying display of electric colors on the back of one's eyelids: phosphenes. And the more he concentrated on the phosphorescent dance of restless photons, the more sense he began to see in it.

The black spots were now small blobs floating in a

brazen sea of fiery gold, a shade of the same intensity as the flames. But the gold was turning molten, bleaching out the warm reds. It was soon no color at all, just a shimmering backdrop of pure heat.

Katz recognized the black dots for what they were: he knew now they were vultures.

Damn Africa!

The year was 1964. . . .


KATZ WATCHED THEM circling lazily in the midday updrafts. Drifting downward, then spiraling away, gliding, waiting all the time, waiting for their grisly feast. But they were in no hurry. For here in the dark heartland of Africa, the vultures always ate their fill.

Katz wiped his forehead and stared again through the field glasses. Nothing! No sign of Nieuwenkamp. The Belgian officer's column should have reached them by now. But the horizon was merely a shimmering empty haze.

He let the binoculars hang on their strap around his neck and glanced over to watch Jo-Jo and his men filling jute sacks with the crumbling reddish earth.

Some things never change.

Like war, for instance.

New and more efficient weapons are devised. The terrain varies from battleground to battleground. But for the fighting man—that poor bastard on the sharp end—much remains constant.

Like the waiting.

And the lousy food.

And the fear.

Not the fear of death itself, because death is the only certainty in this life. It was the haunting anxiety that you could be badly wounded. Maybe so shot up your buddies would have to leave you behind.

Katz watched the men digging in between the withered trees in the old orchards.

This flea-bitten village was called Shogololo.

The place: the south-central border region of the Congo.

The Belgian Congo had barely been granted its independence when the troubles began. Old interests clashed with new ideals; tribe was set against tribe; and the infant African state, rich in resources, was coveted by Marxist dreamers from both within and without.

Tshombe declared Katanga province independent in its own right. But he had no soldiers to back him. Recruiting offices were opened in Johannesburg and Bulawayo, in London and Paris. Hoare, Nieuwenkamp and other top mercenaries rallied to the call, with dozens of men who were ready to serve under these sometimes flamboyant officers.

They struck a new kind of terror into the hearts of their enemies. They became the feared *les Affreux*: the terrible ones. The white brutes of Africa.

It took 20,000 UN troops to stop the mercenaries and put an end to Katanga's bid for independence.

But then, in that summer of 1964, a new rebellion broke out: the Simba Revolt. In Swahili, *simba* means lion; but that was too noble a name for this Communist-backed guerrilla army.

Faced with the growing menace of the Simba uprising, the once-disgraced Prime Minister Tshombe recalled his mercenary friends. Mike Hoare was field commander of the English-speaking Five Commando. The mercenaries soon launched an offensive, spearheading counterattacks to recapture many of the towns and regions seized by the Simbas.

The Simbas wanted one crushing defeat of the foreign forces; one massacre to show that *les Affreux* were not unbeatable. Nieuwenkamp's unit was bearing the brunt of this Simba counterattack.

Katz and his men had been ordered to dig in at Shogololo. If Nieuwenkamp and his men could reach the village they could make a stand there.

"Any sign of them?" asked Delon, climbing up the slope.

"No, nothing yet. Just the vultures," Katz replied. They had about twenty mercs under them, and twice as many native troops. "Everything in place?"

"The mortars are in position. Jo-Jo and his squad are still digging a few more pits. Schneider's got his blacks strung out along the perimeter under those trees."

Delon glanced at his watch. "Scarr should be in position by now."

"How many men did he take with him?"

"Thirty good soldiers. Scarr's young but he's experienced enough to hold the Mbanja Gap."

"By God, I hope so. We're depending on him." Katz started walking back down the slope.

CAPTAIN YAKOV KATZENELENBOGEN was not a common mercenary. French born but raised in Palestine, he was a serving officer in the Israeli army. A senior intelligence official, who had long been keeping an eye on Katz's potential, had had his young protégé drafted for special duties. And now Katz was posing as a soldier of fortune.

The more farsighted among the Israeli command suspected that their future security might lie much in African hands; relatively friendly ones like South Africa, that other beleaguered nation, or in the implacably hostile hands of these newly emerging leaders who expressed their sympathy with the Arab cause. That was why they wanted to know what was happening in the Congo. But behind his cover as an ex-legionnaire, the reason for Katz's presence ran deeper still.

He was on the track of Friedrich Kruger.

The German called himself "Schneider" now. Katz could see him standing over there between the trees, tapping the side of his leg with a rhino-hide fly whisk. He had once been the commander of a Death's Head unit in Eastern Europe. There were others who had methodically disposed of a greater number of Jews and Gypsies, but few who had taken as much pleasure in it. He had earned his title—as the Scourge of Saravansk.

Katz had finally run him to earth in the village of Shogololo. Now this private vendetta must wait as they prepared to make a stand against a mutual enemy.

There had been so much killing. Too much. Katz

had seen men die in skirmishes, ambushes and through plain carelessness. He understood that; he was as well-trained as any man in the soldier's trade. But the butchery did not end there.

An old man had been decapitated in Kasagi for not saying in which direction the Simbas had fled. How could he? He was blind. Automatic fire had shredded two children like rag dolls when they unwisely ran out from their hiding place. A twelve-year-old girl was disemboweled when she refused to submit to the lust of a German mercenary.

Katz was caught up in the killing. He, too, was pulsing with this tropical bloodlust. There was a fever in the air. Katz was certain of it. The savagery of the Congo had infected even him. . . .

"They're coming in!"

It was Jo-Jo who had spotted them first. The wiry black man, Bren gun slung around his shoulder, was standing near the fringe of trees, pointing along the track. It took Katz a few moments to focus on the dark wavery blobs seeming to crawl toward them.

Nieuwenkamp took ten minutes to reach the outskirts of Shogololo. As soon as the two trucks and the armored scout car had passed the old carob tree Delon was using as a range marker, he gave the order to fire.

Delon's mortar fire straddled the track. Dirt, stones and clumps of grass sprouted up along the rutted path. The pursuing Simba jeeps slewed off the road and sought cover.

Major Nieuwenkamp's armored car slowed down in front of the village's only store and the driver sought cover for the vehicle behind a sagging Coca-Cola sign.

Despite the high-speed chase through billowing clouds of African dust, the Belgian officer emerged impeccably dressed. He wore a printed silk scarf knotted around his neck, a plain black beret, and carried an ivory-topped walking cane, which he used more to emphasize his orders than actually for support. Katz had seen him in action and respected his abilities.

"Good to find you here, Captain." His accent was as neatly clipped as his pencil-thin mustache. "What is the situation? Is there a way out?"

The Simbas were regrouping. Jo-Jo saw something move and opened up with his Bren gun.

"The Doushasi road is still open. If we...." Katz was drowned out by the explosions of two incoming shells. One hit the pigsty behind the headman's cottage. Two wounded sows set up a terrible squealing. "If we can stand them off until dark, then the trucks could slip away toward Doushasi. But I must warn you, Major, there have been reports of more Simbas heading through the Mbanja Highlands. Scarr's taken a small force up there to hold the gap."

"Brendan Scarr?" Nieuwenkamp had never trusted the young Afrikaaner.

Katz read the look on the major's face, then shrugged. In this situation they were forced to depend on each other. Every man had a vital role to play. Even Kruger, who was now firing short bursts at anything that moved.

A squad of Simba raiders tried charging up a gully

to the right. One of the mercs, spotting them, waited till the last second and then threw two grenades with pinpoint accuracy.

Another enemy squad had crawled through the longer grass and was trying to reach the alleyway behind the store. They were greeted with broad-bladed bush knives.

Jo-Jo screamed out a warning, pointing to the southwest. Katz could not make out a word; he scanned that sector with his binoculars. Two faint but sizable dust clouds were drifting in the air.

Nieuwenkamp shaded his eyes as he peered into the distance. "It looks as if we'll have our hands full, Captain."

Katz stared disbelievingly. "What the hell happened to Scarr?"

"Dead, probably."

The men under the trees were jumping out of the freshly dug trenches and racing back to find better cover in the village. They had spotted the Simba reinforcements as well.

"Captain, you take some men and...."

Katz anticipated the order and was already moving away when the ground between them exploded in a shrieking cloud of shrapnel and debris.

Katz shook his head, his ears ringing. He did not seem to be seriously hurt.

But Nieuwenkamp was down.

The Israeli sprinted back to his fallen comrade. The major had taken a sliver of shrapnel right through the chest. It had hit him in the back. And his shirt now had a tattered, oozing hole in front.

One of the blacks saw that Nieuwenkamp had been badly wounded. He shouted across to the guy in the next trench. The men knew they could not hold off the Simbas for long.

The blacks started to abandon the orchard in force, retreating in sheer terror.

Katz bundled his bush jacket into a pillow for the dying officer.

The first of the frightened natives raced past Katz. He turned to check the orchard. Kruger, eyes glazed, was leaning out from the cover of a tree.

"Cowards! Scum!" he was screaming at his men.

He brought up his automatic and began firing wildly. Two men were hit. One cartwheeled forward and slammed into a pile of sandbags. The other made jerky motions like a marionette before falling backward into a trench, dead.

Kruger rammed home a fresh magazine, his weapon chattering from the hip as he chased after his fleeing platoon. Three more men went down.

Nieuwenkamp struggled to prop himself up on one elbow. He saw Kruger killing his own troops.

"Katz, get that bastard!" he gasped, grabbing Katz's hand. "You must get...."

He fell back limp.

Nieuwenkamp was dead. Katz did not need his final order for what he was about to do.

Delon came running around the corner of the store. "We can't hold them off much longer. Those other bloody Simbas will be here any minute!"

"Get the trucks started. We'll run for it!" Katz

shouted. He dashed down the street, pulling the Kiwi from its holster.

Kruger saw him coming. He had run out of clips for the submachine gun. He looked right into Katz's eyes and knew that the moment of reckoning had come. Not for shooting the blacks. No, Kruger made the chilling realization he was being called on to account for crimes and atrocities committed far away and long ago.

Katz's temper was controlled. He approached Kruger with icy dispassion. He knew precisely what he was doing. Those cold eyes sent a shiver down Kruger's spine as he recognized the face of his own executioner.

Well, he would take this French Jew-bastard with him! Kruger pulled out a grenade and yanked the pin clear with his teeth. His arm was sweeping forward when Jo-Jo smashed into him.

One powerful black hand crushed the German's fist, holding the grenade fast. They rolled over in the dirt. Kruger started screaming. Too late! Their bodies, locked together for a moment, were blown apart by the explosion.

Katz was knocked to the ground again. This time it felt as if a red-hot claw had ripped into his leg. His pants were shredded around the knee and soaking up a dark red stain.

Kruger, alias Schneider, was literally cut in two.

Katz struggled to stand up, took one look around him, then half ran, half limped toward the truck. Delon was revving it and ready to move. Men were still piling in the back as the Frenchman rammed it into gear.

Madness! Katz shook his head. Bloody madness! The Congo had cost too many good men already. It was not worth it. As the truck roared out of Shogololo, Katz vowed he would never return to this hellish place.

He would leave it to the vultures.

**4**

Bolan admitted Manning to the hotel suite, then resumed his telephone conversation. Manning gestured to the street outside the window. "The car's arrived for us."

Holding his hand cupped over the mouthpiece, Bolan said, "Let them wait. Anyway, April is giving me a geography lesson."

"Are you still with me, John?" said the voice at the other end of the phone, which was not scrambled.

"Of course...go on."

"I was saying that the final result of all the turmoil in the fifties and sixties was that the French Congo became a so-called 'people's republic.' And the Belgian Congo became Zaire. Katanga never did break away, it was just renamed Shaba province. Around the border today lie a handful of pocket-sized states like Rio Muni to the west. And Cabinda, which is under Angolan control. In the east, there's Rwanda and Burundi. Kuranda lies to the south...."

"And it's Kuranda we're interested in?"

"Right. Malakesi, the guy you'll be going to see, was once the minister of justice. He served under Kuranda's first prime minister, Bambabele. His regime was marginally pro-Western, but they were ousted in a coup about five years ago.''

"So who's in charge now?"

"The nominal head of the country is a tribal boy-king called Buka Ntanga. Rumor has it he's retarded. But the real power behind the throne lies with his chief of internal security, the self-appointed General Mumungo.'' April paused for a moment. There was a note of real concern in her voice when she added, ''From the reports we've got, this man makes Idi Amin look like a village priest.''

"What did you get on Brendan Scarr?"

"Half Irish, half Afrikaaner, and totally mean. Been all over the world. Strictly a gun for hire. He was captured in that Angolan mess. For some reason or other they commuted his death sentence. He's doing life in Quita prison.''

"What's the latest entry on him?"

"Two American mercs who finally got back home in a prisoner trade a few months ago reported he was still in there doing his time.''

"And no intelligence updates on Kuranda? Is there a countercoup in the wind?"

"We've no input on that—which is why Hal Brognola would appreciate hearing from you as soon as you've discussed things with Malakesi.''

"Will do, April. And thanks.''

"Any time, Striker, you know that.''

"See you soon.''

"Take care, big man.''

Bolan replaced the receiver. "Okay, Gary, are you ready for a ride?"

Bolan and Manning followed the chauffeur who was standing near the elevator in the lobby. They climbed into the waiting limousine.

THE LINCOLN headed north on the highway out of Toronto.

The massive high-rise apartments were quickly left behind. The big car quit the freeway and the urban landscape gave way to fields covered with patches of snow on both sides of the road. Bolan surveyed the Ontario scenery with detached interest.

They crested a low hill and the chauffeur slowed to a crawl. A beige Chevrolet was parked on the soft shoulder. The driver was smoking a cigarette while his companion dozed with a hat pulled over his eyes. They looked like a couple of salesmen taking a break from their calls. Bolan and Manning exchanged glances; neither of them believed that for a moment.

Up ahead on the left was a thick cluster of tall evergreens, evidently planted to afford privacy to the large house set back from the road. The chauffeur drove the big car through the tall hedge that flanked the curve of the graveled drive. The car pulled to a halt in front of a mock-Tudor mansion.

The driver slipped smartly from the car and opened the rear door for the visitors.

Bolan and Manning walked up the steps and rang the doorbell. The door was opened by a distinguished-looking black man in a business suit.

"Good morning, gentlemen."

"Good morning. I'm John Phoenix, and this is my associate, Gary Manning."

"And I am Malakesi." Bolan placed the accent as that of a top British boarding school. It was the same voice he had heard on the phone that morning.

The man motioned them to follow him through the main hall. "It is very good of you to come at such short notice."

"Your proposition—what little we know of it—intrigued us," Bolan replied candidly.

"Good," said Malakesi. "Perhaps you gentlemen would like some refreshments?"

"Coffee will be fine," said Bolan. Manning nodded in agreement.

Malakesi seemed about to launch into a more detailed explanation for this meeting when a middle-aged man wearing an open khaki shirt walked into the lounge. He advanced on Bolan with hand outstretched.

"Colonel John Phoenix," Malakesi began his introduction in measured tones, "this is Prime Minister Andrew—"

"—Bambabele," Bolan completed the formalities.

"You recognize me," said Bambabele. Although he had recently reemerged on the foreign-news pages, he still managed to sound pleasantly surprised. He gripped Bolan's elbow and gave him a firm, dry handshake. "You follow the news?"

"Professional interest," conceded Bolan. He quoted: "Andrew Bambabele, ex-prime minister of Kuranda, has left the Caribbean and is now believed to be staying with friends in the vicinity of Toronto. I think that's how *Time* reported it."

"Correct and properly vague." Bambabele gave an approving nod.

"Do the powers-that-be know you're here?"

"You must have passed their sentries on the way in."

"Of course," said Bolan, referring to the two men in the beige Chevy. "We spotted the welcoming committee."

"To tell the truth, I'm not sure if they're posted out there for my protection or to keep me under surveillance for their own government."

"A little of both, I imagine."

"Even after five years of exile, the powers-that-be, as you called them, still remain alert to the slightest shift in the winds of world opinion." Bambabele made an expansive gesture with his hands. "If they find they can live comfortably with the new regime, they will make disapproving noises and swear they're doing their very best to deport me. But, following the latest reports of Mumungo's outrages, I seem to be gaining international sympathy once more, so I expect that soon they will announce I am at last being granted political asylum."

"Thus gaining diplomatic leverage," added Bolan.

"Precisely, Colonel. Liberals of the Western world cannot be satisfied with simply acting liberally... they must be seen to do so, and then patted on the back for living up to their, um, principles."

To Mack Bolan, such honesty was refreshing.

"I ought not to sound so cynical," added the ex-prime minister, though without any trace of apology. "But let us discuss the proposition I have for you."

Bambabele served himself a gin and tonic, then nodded toward his aide. "Mr. Malakesi has already spoken to the person in Washington you gave him as a professional reference. You and your associates come with the highest recommendations. But let us waste no more time.

"I—that is, we, the people of Kuranda—would be indebted to you, Colonel, if you would lead a small patrol into our country, there to retrieve something that now morally belongs to us all, and bring it back out."

Both Bambabele and Malakesi watched their guests' faces closely, but neither man betrayed any emotion other than a curiosity for more specific details.

"Kuranda was born out of the division of the equatorial colonies. For several years it was the battleground of more or less legally constituted armies, guerrillas, the United Nations and *les Affreux*."

Bolan nodded; this much he already knew.

Bambabele continued. "When the Simba Revolt swept over what is now the borders of Kuranda, the mercenaries fought a dozen courageous actions. In one small battle, a South African volunteer named Brendan Scarr abandoned the position he was supposed to be defending in the Mbanja Highlands and with two dozen or so men raided the nearby town of Tshilanga. They shot up the place, and in the ensuing confusion they robbed the local bank. Stripped it

clean! Barely ahead of the Simbas, they escaped with
the loot through the bush country to the northwest.
About two weeks later, Scarr reappeared alone,
empty-handed but in one piece, having paddled down
the Makala and Kasai rivers to safety. It must be
assumed that he killed all his men, presumably after
burying the loot.''

"And this is what you want us to recover?" asked
Manning.

"The town Scarr raided had been the base of
operations for a man called Willem Vandergriff,''
said Bambabele, ignoring Manning's question.

The name meant nothing to Bolan.

"Vandergriff,'' explained Malakesi, "was probably the most notorious diamond smuggler in all of
west-central Africa. It was he who controlled
that bank and used it to store the bulk of his illicit
stock."

Things were beginning to make sense to Manning.
"So Scarr must have got away with quite a haul in
uncut diamonds."

"Yes," confirmed Bambabele. "Vandergriff was
stockpiling a private hoard of stones that today
would be worth more than five million dollars."

So it was to be a treasure hunt after all, thought
Bolan. Would it be worth risking the lives of Phoenix
Force to recover a few boxes of precious stones?

"There's something else I must tell you," continued Bambabele, almost as if he could sense
Bolan's growing reluctance to get involved. "Unknown to either Vandergriff or Scarr, a man named
Asiwa, the manager of the Tshilanga bank, was the

key figure in organizing the movement that helped bring me to power. All the paperwork that coordinated our separatist movement and the liaison work with American agents was kept in one of the deposit boxes stolen by Scarr.''

Now Bolan was interested. Very interested.

"Yes, Colonel, papers that could implicate American agents and other, even more unorthodox agents working for the West. Even after all this time, the names and the details must not fall into the wrong hands.''

"What happened to Asiwa?'' asked Manning.

"He was killed in the bank raid.''

"And the diamond smuggler?''

"Willem Vandergriff survived until a few years ago, when he died in Switzerland.''

"Why didn't Scarr ever collect his loot?'' asked Manning.

"For a long time he was kept on the run by men who Vandergriff hired to track him down. Scarr always managed to elude them. Then came the fighting for Angola in 1976. Scarr saw it as his one chance to recover the diamonds, by crossing over the border into Kuranda and making his way back to the upper reaches of the Makala.''

"But things didn't work out for him, did they?''

"No, Colonel, they didn't.'' Bambabele smiled. "This time the mercenaries were so badly organized that they were routed by the Marxist guerrillas. Scarr was among those taken prisoner and put on trial. He has been serving a life sentence in Quita prison.''

"Has been?''

"We still have an underground network sympathetic to our cause, and it has informed us that Scarr has struck a deal for his freedom. The Russians have sent in a new 'adviser,' Colonel Yagoda."

"And Scarr has made a bargain with this Yagoda?"

"Yes, according to our sources he is preparing to lead a long-range patrol across Kuranda to recover the treasure."

The final piece of the puzzle was now in place.

"And you want us to be there when they fetch it, is that it?" Bolan lit a cigarette. "You want my team to rob the robbers, as it were?"

"Exactly, Colonel. As soon as Scarr and his men have located the loot, then you would step in and relieve them of it."

"If you... *when* you succeed," said Malakesi, "it will be a decisive blow against any further interference by the Angolans, together with their Russian and Cuban masters. It will also make General Mumungo, whose own position grows precarious, into a laughingstock. He is, after all, supposedly in charge of internal security."

"And the proceeds from the diamonds would help finance your own return to power."

"Yes," agreed Bambabele. "But if you should fail, then not only would a wealth of uncut stones fall into the wrong hands, but they will discover the papers and the Kremlin will ensure that secret American involvement in African affairs is publicized around the world."

"Many of the people named in those documents

are dead by now," admitted Malakesi. "Some of us escaped after the coup. Others, less fortunate, have been executed. But there was a large cadre that wisely chose to lie low over the years. They made little of the vital role they played in the birth of Kuranda, but even now they form the backbone of what resistance there is to Ntanga and Mumungo. If they should be uncovered, Colonel. . .it won't be a purge, it will be a bloodbath."

The longer-range strategic implications were clear to Bolan. The United States would lose its one opportunity to help reestablish a friendly power in a decidedly unfriendly part of the world.

"I beg you, Colonel Phoenix, to accept this commission."

"Hard to refuse," said Bolan, rising to shake the ex-prime minister's hand on it, "when the Kremlin's involved."

"DID BAMBABELE mention INGOT?" Brognola asked Bolan over the phone later that evening.

"No, he didn't say where the money was coming from. He left it to Malakesi to talk over the financial end. They've raised a quarter of a million for the job. They'll get a good return on their investment if we bring back the diamonds."

"Since they don't know you like I do, Striker, what's to stop you from running off with the loot?"

"Malakesi made it quite clear there was an emergency fund that would be posted on our heads if we tried anything like that."

Brognola chuckled as he tried to imagine any

bounty hunter who would live to collect it. "I think INGOT put up the money. They're an international mining consortium that lost their concessions in Kuranda when Bambabele was kicked out."

Brognola did not need to point out how much INGOT stood to gain by having a prime minister back in power who looked favorably on their own goals. More vested interests!

"Do you think he's right about these papers, Hal?"

"Yes, I do. Damn right. Even if Asiwa's lists and information are old hat, the KGB and their unwitting friends among the Western media will have a heyday exposing our past connections in Africa."

"Not to mention what it'll mean for the future."

"Quite. There'll be another bloody purge and then we'll have lost our one best chance of gaining an ally in central Africa. And it's quite in the cards that we could be drawn into another 'peacekeeping' role— this time on the Angolan border region. Sure, it's a low-intensity conflict area right now, at least officially...but it could explode at any moment. And any chance the Reds have to stir up shit in that part of the world will not be wasted."

"So the papers are more important than the diamonds—to both sides?"

Brognola was silent for a moment. "Yes, we must get those documents. But you'll get no orders from the top. If any of you get caught inside Kuranda... well, you're on your own. Any connections would be denied."

That was standard operating procedure. Bolan

knew that. But Brognola felt uneasy enough to emphasize the point.

"You'll be branded as international adventurers. And Washington will have to agree."

"I understand."

Phoenix Force would be on their own in the Congo hellzone.

But this time The Executioner was leading them.

5

Bolan ground out his cigarette in the dirt. He stood there silently savoring the last of the tropical twilight. The suddenness with which it melted into velvet darkness amazed him.

The moon was young: just a cold crescent of silver hanging over this ancient land. Bolan took a deep breath—satisfaction mixed with anticipation. Tomorrow night would be perfect for the drop.

The twin beams of Sorbara's jeep probed along the dusty track around the far perimeter of the field. McCarter and Ohara would arrive shortly. Then all the members of Phoenix Force would be here.

Bolan strode back toward the hangar and pushed open the wicket door. The cavernous building was harshly lit by four work lamps. For a moment their direct glare was shielded from him by the shadowy bulk of the aircraft parked in the center of the oil-stained floor. The venerable Otter seemed improbably large within these confines.

Bolan reached up to pat the wing strut as he walked over to the workbench where most of the weaponry was laid out.

Gary Manning was sitting cross-legged on a patch

of canvas, reassembling the detonator he had just checked out down to the last screw.

Rafael Encizo, the deadly Cuban contribution to Bolan's team, was inspecting each primer closely before placing it securely in a protective case.

Steve Hohenadel, the pilot, heard the sound of the vehicle pulling up on the tarmac outside and nodded at the American leader.

Only Katz did not look around. He remained staring at the map of central Africa that was tacked over a schedule of flying lessons on the large bulletin board. A cigarette smoldered in the corner of his mouth; its ash had acquired a perilous droop. Bolan thought he looked weary and bitter in the brightness of those naked bulbs, and he watched as Katz rubbed the back of his glove as if his right hand was still encased by it.

Chris Sorbara came in first, followed by David McCarter and Keio Ohara.

"Any problems?" Hohenadel asked Sorbara.

"No. Johnny Scarlip was a little curious about what I was doing back in town, but I took the scenic route out and left him behind."

Hohenadel seemed satisfied. It wasn't too hard to shake off the customary Central Intelligence Organization—CIO—tail, especially a lazy bastard like old Johnny Scarlip. Nkomo himself was no longer a threat, but Zimbabwe's leader still had his hands full trying to put down the challenge presented by the followers of his rival, Matabele. There were too many so-called allies ready to eat his Marxist ass for Mugabe's secret police to follow every white businessman or tourist who stopped off in Salisbury.

Each member of Phoenix Force had entered the country under a different tailor-made cover; in each case, preventive measures had been taken to ensure no snoop from the CIO would track them to their rendezvous at the bush airstrip, two hours' drive from the capital.

"Colonel, you have my undying gratitude," announced McCarter. "Your summons has saved me from a fate worse than death!"

It was Manning who raised an inquiring eyebrow.

"Hell hath no fury like a woman scorned," explained the Englishman.

"Well, since we're trading clichés," replied Bolan, "you might be jumping out of the frying pan and into the fire."

McCarter grinned. It was precisely the kind of action he looked forward to; in fact, the ex-SAS officer thrived on it.

"Yakov, how are you?" McCarter's gesture was part wave, part salute, and wholly respectful. He had never forgotten the lesson that the older man had taught him at their first encounter, when McCarter had churlishly addressed him as "dads."

Keio Ohara seemed to almost glide across the floor. Years of self-discipline and rigorous training in the martial arts had given him a self-assurance and grace of movement that few men ever achieve.

The lighthearted banter with which the warriors greeted each other belied their utter dedication to the cause Mack Bolan had rallied them to; for beneath this casual veneer they were fighting men devoted to the destruction of evil wherever it might be found.

"There's still much to do, gentlemen, and no time to waste," said Bolan, stepping in front of the map. He pointed to the area of the airfield and then traced a course to the northwest, across Zambia and up along the eastern border of Angola. His finger stopped its path and he tapped a spot on the map.

"This is our target: Kuranda. A patrol of MPLA troopers, probably with some Cuban surrogates riding herd, is about to enter Kuranda and attempt to reach this region, the headwaters of the Makala River. The patrol is under the command of one Colonel Yagoda, fresh from Moscow if our intelligence is correct. He is guided by a South African called Brendan Scarr. The object of their expedition is to retrieve a cache of loot that Scarr left behind years ago. Our objective, men, is to take it away from them."

McCarter's teeth flashed in a tight grin—yes, this was going to be right up his street!

Bolan signaled to Katz, who now stepped forward.

"Because of my familiarity with the region," began the ex-Mossad agent, "Colonel Phoenix has asked me to say a few words about the terrain we'll be operating in, and about the guide Colonel Phoenix mentioned before, Brendan Scarr. Quite honestly I'm not sure which is more dangerous."

There was a venom in his tone that made even Manning stop wiping his hands on the rag he held.

"Basically this eastern edge of Kuranda can be divided into three regions. In the south, where we'll be landing, it's rolling grasslands. It used to be a pocket of big-game country and it's still relatively unpopulated. The only feasible point of entry for Scarr and his gang is through the Mbanja Gap. Heading northeast they'll hit a long strip of very hostile drylands. It's a small desert caused by the rainshadow of the Mambosso Range. I warn you, it isn't known as the Devil's Forge for nothing.''

Bolan caught Hohenadel exchanging an uneasy glance with his partner. The two pilots were obviously glad they had only the delivery and pick-up details to attend to—there was no way they wanted to trek across the Forge.

"Here in the top corner of Kuranda," Katz continued, "the land rises quickly. Steep hills and gorges are clad in semitropical rain forest. Difficult country. And this is where the Makala begins. It's where Scarr is probably heading. . . he buried the loot somewhere in that godforsaken jungle.''

Bolan scanned each of the men who made up Phoenix Force. They were concentrating entirely on Katz's preliminary briefing.

"Some years ago—1964 to be exact—during one of the many crises in the Congo, Scarr deserted the post he'd been entrusted to defend for a little private enterprise of his own. He was willing to profit at the cost of other men's lives. It's up to us to write the final figures on the balance sheet.''

There was no mistaking Katz's intention: this time Brendan Scarr was going to end up in the red!

Bolan spoke next. "I'll fill in further details with each of you later, and we'll discuss specific assignments. Right now I want to introduce you officially to Steve Hohenadel and Chris Sorbara—they'll be flying us in and out on this job.''

Hohenadel put down the half-empty bottle of beer he was holding, ambled to the front and touched the long peak of his Five Star Oil baseball cap. He and Sorbara had been picked by the Stony Man computer as the best local men for the job. Both of them were highly experienced African bush pilots who had shown exceptional dedication to the cause of civilized order in the protracted war for Rhodesia.

"Hi, I'm Steve...this is my partner and copilot, Chris. He's coming along to spell me at the controls and shut the hatch after you've jumped. Behind you is the *Amelia*. She's a De Havilland DHC-3. Amphibian, as you can see. Ex-Ghana air force. Ex-mail plane running the Mozambique Channel. Now she belongs to Chris and me—or at least she will after three more payments."

Although the two fliers obviously had a vested interest in the safe return of their craft, McCarter had an important question. "The only time I flew an Otter, I remember its range was limited to under a thousand miles."

"Normally that's correct but longer-range fuel tanks were added," explained Hohenadel. "It should be able to cover around fourteen hundred miles with this payload aboard."

McCarter glanced at the map, then back to Hohenadel. "Ah, yes. But that isn't going to get us to Kuranda, is it? Are we supposed to walk the rest of the way?"

"We'll take it in two legs," replied the pilot, pointing to a spot a little more than halfway to the intended drop zone. "We'll touch down here: Lake Kalambasse. It's been arranged with friendlies to refuel us there. After you've jumped, we'll return to Kalambasse and wait there for you. Seventy-two hours is the time limit. You've got to be in and out within three days.''

''And how do we accomplish that?'' asked Ohara.

''Ground support has been arranged through the facilities of a large mining consortium.'' Bolan picked up the briefing. ''No names, no pack drill. But we'll be met at the drop point by Luke Rawson, a surveyor, who'll bring us transport and act as the local guide. After we've hit Scarr's mob, it'll be up to Rawson to get us aboard a float plane to fly us out to Kalambasse and our rendezvous with the *Amelia.*''

STEVE HOHENADEL opened the throttle smoothly. The Otter rolled forward. He gave it just a touch of right rudder, felt the elevators come alive, trimmed the plane, and then rose so effortlessly that they were in the air before his passengers had noticed the lift-off.

McCarter was impressed. Each man had his own special contribution to make. It would be up to McCarter to fly them out of Kuranda. If they made it.

The rest of Phoenix Force were thinking of their individual responsibilities. Encizo and Manning were discussing tricks for setting explosives. Katz and Bolan were looking at a larger-scale map of the drop zone, a deserted stretch of bush several miles north of a village named Shogololo.

''Kuranda will be a better place when Bambabele's back in power,'' mused Katz.

"I'm not going for Bambabele," said Bolan. "It's the papers that are important."

The older man paused for a moment before wondering aloud: "I wonder what sort of a cut INGOT are going to get from the diamonds."

Bolan shrugged. They had to get them first.

Encizo leaned forward: "Why don't we land right there on the river?"

"The Makala?" Katz shook his head. "Impossible. It's a roaring torrent through those upper gorges. Thick with copper-bearing sludge. The natives call it the 'River of Blood.' Couldn't get the plane down there."

"Besides, we don't know exactly where Scarr is heading for," added Bolan  'No, we have to cut their trail here in the south, playing Tail-end Charlie while they lead us to the cache."

"Think there could be any trouble from the Kuranda Air Force?" asked Encizo.

"It's not worth spit," Bolan told him. "And the latest reports indicated that Mumungo has all his forces concentrated in the western sector anyway, mostly around the capital. He needs a show of air strength to stay in power."

Manning scanned the sky off the port wing. "What about along this border, Colonel?"

"Mugabe's got troubles of his own. Saboteurs have wiped out nearly half his air force. A dozen Hunters, Hawks and a Cessna all got blown up on the ground. Zimbabwe doesn't have enough air power to check out every tourist flight."

Hohenadel steered a course west by south, as if

they were on a routine overflight of Victoria Falls, but then he swung ninety degrees to starboard and cut across the corner of Zambia. Sometimes rising for cloud cover, but mostly using his extensive knowledge of the ground contours, the Rhodesian pilot flew on toward Kuranda undetected.

"Want some coffee?" Manning offered the thermos to Encizo, who shook his head. The Canadian passed it back to Ohara, who also declined.

Hohenadel and Sorbara had proved as good at quartermastering as they were at flying. Years of internal strife had left Africa awash in arms. Guns were expensive, but they had managed to supply Bolan and his men with more than adequate firepower.

Bolan had a familiar M-16, fitted with a sniper scope. Ohara took the Armalite with a grenade launcher attached. Manning and McCarter both had FNs, and Encizo cradled a Czech-made Skorpion.

The Uzi was left for Katz. It was an older model with a scarred wooden stock, but well cared for; the Israeli soldier felt comfortable with it. Anyway, Katz was always armed. Built into the titanium steel finger of his artificial hand was a single-shot .22 Magnum. Very effective at close range.

The team carried an assortment of .45s and .357 handguns, explosives, fragmentation and smoke grenades and enough ammunition to start a small war.

THAT UNEASY MOMENT before jumping into the unknown darkness was relieved by the fact that each man was glad to be getting out of the cramped quarters of the aircraft.

It had been a tedious flight. They had stopped on the placid waters of Kalambasse no longer than it took to refuel the Otter. But still they were twenty minutes later than Hohenadel's estimated time of arrival. The two pilots would be lucky to make it back to their lakeshore hideout before it was light.

Bolan took a deep breath to steady himself. A static line had been rigged for the low-level jump, but there had been no point in fixing up the customary green and red lights for this jump. Keio, who had taken paracommando training, was the jumpmaster. He would be the last to drop through the floor hatch. Bolan was going first.

"Three...two...one," Hohenadel called out from the controls.

Sorbara tapped Keio on the shoulder. "This is it."

Ohara's narrowed eyes glinted with excitement. "Go!"

Bolan levered himself forward and dropped through the open hatch.

The clear cold wind stripped away the stuffiness of the flight. Bolan could hear the chute streaming out above his head as the plane droned steadily away from him.

There was no sickening lurch as the dark silk umbrella mushroomed above him, just a gentle tug as he swung upright, his hands automatically reaching for the toggles. Against the glittering starry backdrop, Bolan could make out the other black silhouettes billowing down.

He spilled a little air from the chute, turning into the breeze to cut his lateral speed. There were no lights below to pick out the landing zone. Even as he scanned across the pitch-black grassland for a sign of Rawson, Bolan's feet struck the ground and he rolled forward.

Within seconds the commander was gathering the parachute's fabric into a tight ball. The equipment would have to be buried here. No sign of their arrival must be left visible for some inquisitive native to report.

Click-clack!

The sharp metallic sound off to his right was from Katz. A second signal followed from farther away. The team was gathering together.

Manning loomed out of the darkness, carrying his chute bundled under his arm. Encizo and Ohara, lugging the supplies container, closed in on Bolan.

"No reception committee," grunted the Canadian. "Hope to hell we're in the right place."

"Think we must be." McCarter's voice was surprisingly close. "I landed right in the middle of the bloody road!"

The "road" was nothing more than two closely parallel tracks beaten into the dry earth.

The *Amelia* had vanished. Bolan and his men had landed in the very heart of the African killing ground. And they were quite alone.

**6**

Dawn broke with the same startling shock as the tropical twilight had vanished. The night sky split apart along the seam of the horizon. A faint gray lilac smudge was momentarily streaked with pink, then the red gold rim of the sun erupted over the distant folds of the withered savanna.

The rainy season should have begun already, but the climate of the African wilderness had become erratic in the past few years. There was a bright yellow flash overhead as a weaverbird flew southward in search of a water hole.

"I knew we'd end up walking!" said McCarter.

"The exercise will do you good," Manning shot back. "Quit grumbling and give me a hand."

The ordnance had been distributed. Their ammo pouches were full. The explosives and detonating equipment stood on the grass in their cases. And the parachutes had been bundled together into the empty container.

Hearing McCarter's good-natured gripe, Bolan looked across as the two men lowered the capsule into the pit they had dug. Manning was dressed much as he had been for Clayton's war game. But this time, thank God, it was for real. The others also all wore some combination of jungle-patterned fatigues.

Katz was staring down the track that eventually joined the Doushasi road outside Shogololo. He knew why he had come back to the Congo, but he was still uneasy. This whole damn operation had been mounted in too much of a hurry.

"If we don't get transport soon we're going to lose them," he said. Katz hadn't come this far to miss Scarr. "Unless there was a mistake—maybe they haven't crossed the border yet."

Bolan shook his head. There had been no mistake. He had listened to the message himself, patched through to the radio shack at the airstrip. It was brief and to the point: "The visitors have arrived." One of Bambabele's spies had spotted the Angolan unit approaching the Mbanja Gap. His report had crackled through static halfway around the world and back again.

"They're here all right," said Bolan. "I can feel it. My bet is they'll be resting up during the daylight hours."

"Traveling only at night?" Katz said. "Yes, I agree. What if we...."

Keio waggled his hand, signaling for quiet. "Vehicle approaching! Sounds like a tank."

Manning tamped the last of the fresh dirt over the hole and covered it with a clump of dry grass, then cupped one hand to his ear to listen.

"Yes." Bolan turned to the others. "Two vehicles. Okay, men, head for cover. Safeties off, but wait on my order."

Keio had already vanished into the grass. Katz and Encizo crouched behind a thorn bush. Bolan quickly checked to see they had left no signs of disturbance on the ground, then he faded into the scrub.

There was a flickering movement between the trunks of a clump of thorn trees, then a Land Rover swung into view. It was moving slowly and kicking up very little dust. The white man standing on the passenger side patted the black driver on the shoulder. They stopped and through field glasses the man methodically checked the bush stretching away on both sides of the track.

Nothing out there.... The man spat in the dirt and gave a second signal for his driver to begin crawling forward again. An old truck appeared, following the first vehicle at two hundred yards. It sounded as if the exhaust system was in bad shape. Now they were close enough for Bolan to read the half-obliterated company name stenciled on the side: Afric Ore Extraction.

He stood up and took three paces to the edge of the track. The driver stamped on the brakes so suddenly that his passenger lurched forward against the top of the windshield.

"Jesus, Kambolo! Watch what you're...." He stopped berating the driver and stared suspiciously at the stranger standing about thirty feet in front of them.

"Mr. Rawson?" the battle-ready newcomer inquired.

"Yes, that's me." He looked relieved. "You must be Phoenix."

"You're late, Mr. Rawson. We expected to find you here waiting for us."

Without a sound, Phoenix Force emerged from their hiding places. Rawson glanced round open-mouthed. Five more men. Big men. And armed to the teeth. Rawson always figured there wasn't much that escaped him in the bush, but these guys came out of nowhere, as silent as snakes.

Kambolo sat impassively behind the wheel. Nothing that happened out here could surprise him. Mercenaries, UN troops, the Congolese army, and Mumungo's soldiers—Kambolo had seen them all.

"We got here as fast as we could," Rawson claimed. He turned around and signaled to the second driver to creep forward and close the gap. "Had a problem with the truck."

"What sort of problem?" snapped Katz, feeling a warning prickle at the back of his neck.

"Oil leak. Don't worry, it's fixed. Wouldn't come out here without spares for everything." His thin mouth compressed and the creases around his eyes bunched tighter. Rawson appeared a little indignant that he should have to offer an explanation. His eyes darted back and forth from the tall Oriental to the older man to the silent, Hispanic-looking guy.

In the city, Rawson's wary look might have been thought of as shifty, but in these circumstances he just seemed cautious and watchful.

"You can call me Luke. Kambolo here is my driver. The fellow driving the truck is Mulanda." The second black nodded from the open window of his cab. "He's Mussengamba—best damn trackers there are! He'll help us find the game."

Bolan stared hard at Rawson. Very hard. Bolan thought of his foes as rats or vermin or the treacherous animals they so closely resembled, but never as "game." This was anything but a sport. His men were not here on a Sunday afternoon safari.

Rawson shifted uncomfortably. "So...'the visitors' have arrived?"

"That was the report."

"Well, they won't risk staying on this track. No telling who they might run into, eh?" Rawson looked around him. Encizo and Ohara were already loading their gear into the trucks. These guys were not wasting any time. "No, they'll probably travel through the bush on a parallel course."

"They've still got to head for the Devil's Forge."

Rawson spat again at Bolan's mention of that hellish desert. He made a circling movement with his left arm. "I suggest we make a sweep back out to the west. See if we can spot some sign. Mulanda's got some of his Mussengamba relatives out there. He can find out what they've seen."

Bolan signaled for Manning to sit with him in the Land Rover. Katz ordered the others into the mining-company truck and climbed up into the back with them.

"Okay, let's go!"

KATZ WAS GLAD to be riding in the truck. He did not like Rawson. This whole assignment had started out on the wrong foot for him. But he did not let it show.

John Phoenix might be calling the shots on this mission, but he, Katz, was still leader of the team.

"Are those primers secure?" he asked Encizo, rather more sharply than he had intended. He tipped his head toward the case that was wedged between the food boxes and tents that Rawson had brought for the expedition. The truck was bouncing badly over the rutted path through a low thicket of thorny scrub.

"Checked them myself," nodded the swarthy Cuban. He pointed to some movement in the bush. "What's that?"

Katz balanced himself against the cover frame and tried to steady the field glasses in his good hand. "Lionesses. Starting the day's hunt."

The endless cycle of life and death on the African savanna had begun for yet another day. Once more the predators were on the prowl.

The big tawny cats in the distance stalked an unwary wildebeest. A pack of jackals followed at a respectful distance, hoping that they, too, would get their fill. Overhead, the vultures circled.

It made no difference to the vultures what they feasted on.

And across this savage land man hunted man.

GARY MANNING GLANCED BACK through the choking haze to see how well the truck was keeping up. One more of these potholes and that muffler was likely to fall right off. Manning decided he'd take a look at it himself the next time Colonel Phoenix called a halt.

They had spotted lions, hyenas, antelope and wild

dogs—once Bolan thought he had caught a glimpse
of an elephant in the distance—but no trace at all of
Scarr's patrol. At one point they took a short break
while Mulanda scouted out a village alone. But there
was no news of strangers in the vicinity.

Bolan kept a ceaseless vigil, constantly sweeping
the endless yellow, brown and dusty green landscape.
They were out there somewhere. He knew it.

"So Scarr's come back for his treasure?" Rawson
was only trying to make conversation, but Bolan
didn't like the way he zeroed in directly on the goal of
this mission. Just how well had their guide been
briefed? And by whom, wondered Bolan.

"What makes you say that?"

"Why else would Scarr risk his neck coming back
here?" Rawson turned to display a reassuring grin
"Hell, everybody and his dog has heard of Scarr's
treasure. Gold bars, diamonds, rubies.... There's
a mountain of the stuff, if you believe all the
rumors."

"And what do you think?"

"Like I said, it's all gossip." Their escort
shrugged. "If Scarr knocked over the Tshilanga bank
he'd have been lucky to get the deeds to a few proper-
ties, some stocks and bonds maybe, and some loose
change. He's a fool to come back for.... Kambolo,
stop!"

The driver touched the brake pedal twice to flash a
warning light to the truck, then pulled to a halt.

Manning stood up in the back. "What did you
see?"

"Nothing. It's what I smell."

Bolan had already caught the scent and was scanning the sector windward.

"Got it. There!" He pointed to a faint dirty smudge drifting above the trees a couple of miles away.

Kambolo drove the most direct route he could, the Land Rover bucking in the uneven terrain, but it still took nearly ten minutes to reach the place marked by the smoke.

The acrid odor of smoldering thatch lingered on the breeze. And there was another sickly, sweeter smell. It had been in a different part of the world that Bolan had first been acquainted with that peculiar scent. There was no mistaking it: the stench of charred human flesh.

## 7

The wheels of the jeep spat out angry spumes of reddish grit as Kambolo trod on the accelerator. He steered straight for the low huddle of straw-thatched huts, smashing through the last of the low brush, then plowing across the corner of a dried-up corn patch.

Bolan and Manning were ready for anything. Their weapons traversed to cover both sides of the vehicle as they roared into the village square.

The jeep skidded to a halt.

It must have been a poor-looking place at the best of times. But this was the worst of times. Ashes still swirled about the beaten-earth compound as the breeze plucked them from two of the ruined hovels on the far side of the street.

Thirty feet in front of the jeep a woman knelt in the dirt, cradling the limp corpse of an old man in her arms. The gaily colored cotton wrap she wore, a *pagne*, was streaked with grime and bloodstains. Her mouth hung open as her shoulders shook with dry, half-strangulated sobs.

Manning leaped from the back of the Land Rover and ran forward, but there was nothing he could do. The old man had been slit open from his crotch to his throat. Manning touched the woman gently on the shoulder, but she would not be comforted.

Bolan had crossed the street. Another body, that of a younger man, hung by the wrists from the lowest branch of a nearby tree. His back was lacerated. White points of bone poked through the gaping slashes that crisscrossed his ebony skin. He had been flayed by an expert. The swarming flies buzzed indignantly at being disturbed as Bolan sliced through the bindings that held the victim.

Wrists freed, the man's body dropped first to its knees, then toppled face forward. The cloud of flies settled back onto the corpse again.

Bolan tucked the K-bar back into its ankle sheath and straightened up as the truck pulled in behind the Land Rover. Ohara waited for the vehicle to stop before he swung himself up onto the roof of the cab to stand watch.

"Check those hooches," ordered Bolan. McCarter and Encizo began a fast but thorough house-by-house search along the edge of the square.

Katz paused at the end of the empty corral. A man—or what was left of him—was lashed to a weathered post. The fire that had been lit between his legs still glowed faintly. The flesh on his thighs, genitals and lower stomach was a roasted, suppurating mess. The flies feasted on the blackened sockets of his eyes. His head twitched once as he made an obscene gurgle. It only took a single shot from the Uzi to dispatch the villager from his agony.

The Israeli commando walked on to join Bolan. His expression was grim.

"Ask her who did this," Bolan instructed Mulanda. These people were Nabu, a subtribe of the Bantu, but the black tracker knew enough of the local dialect to question the woman.

She said nothing. Her eyes rolled upward piteously and her head lolled back and forth as she soulfully denied the ugly reality of what had happened to her home and family. It was apparent she would be of little use to them.

Rawson and his driver were inspecting the tracks at the far end of the street.

"Find anything?" Bolan called out. It could not have been more than an hour, maybe much less, since this massacre took place. He wanted to know precisely what they were up against.

Even as the mining surveyor shrugged a negative reply, Manning yelled, "Look out!"

The sound had come from a hut right behind the American commander.

Katz whirled, finger on the trigger, the Uzi gripped in his good left hand like a pistol. He had only one split second to ease off the pressure and let the muzzle sag toward the ground.

Standing in the open doorway was a shaven-headed youngster, no more than eight or nine, with flies clustered in the corners of his eyes and under his runny nose. He kept blinking in bewilderment. Bolan realized the boy must have been hidden away before the killing began.

Mulanda said something to the kid.

The boy slowly shook his head.

"I told him we've just arrived," explained the

tracker, "and we're trying to find out what happened here. I don't think he believes me."

Who could blame him, thought Katz.

Seeing that the moment's excitement was over, McCarter resumed his patrol. The next *rondeval* was partially gutted. Its roof had caved in and the smoke-blackened mud walls had crumbled. He stood at the entrance, surveying the debris. The lumpy outline half-buried in the ashes seemed to indicate a small dog or pig had got caught in the fire.

The Englishman moved closer to the spot. It was not the remains of any animal—it was a baby!

McCarter turned away, sickened by the savagery, and that was when he saw the man.

"Hey, you!" McCarter yelled at the figure lurking in a corner of the last hut in the row. He had been there long enough to see half a dozen foreign soldiers prowling around the ruins of his village: the ghosts of *les Affreux* had come back to the Congo!

At the sound of McCarter's voice the man started to run for his life.

McCarter's challenge had alerted the others. Ohara swung around and brought the Armalite to bear. Bolan waved for him not to shoot, although from Ohara's vantage point he could draw a clear bead on the fleeing figure. Mulanda jumped behind the wheel of the Land Rover as Bolan vaulted in from the other side.

The tracker gunned the jeep as he set off in hot pursuit.

The running man had less than three hundred

yards head start and that was quickly being narrowed. The dried stalks of the old corn plants whipped at his powerful legs as he raced toward the cover of the nearest scrub.

Mulanda's face was a mask of concentration as the four-wheel-drive vehicle hit the lip of a deep rut and bounced high. He was coming up fast on the left.

Bolan poised to make his leap. Mulanda closed the gap. Their quarry tried to swerve away sharply to the right. Too late! The big soldier launched himself in a flying tackle.

Two hundred pounds of muscle and bone slammed into the man like a ton of bricks. They both crashed to the ground, sliding forward in a tangled, scrapping heap. The black had been winded by the impact and there was now little fight left in him.

Bolan quickly overpowered him. He twisted the villager's arm behind his back and propelled him toward the Land Rover.

"Get in!"

Mulanda repeated the instruction in Nabu.

Bolan unholstered his Beretta, but the man sat quietly in the seat, his shoulders set in a sullen slump. Powerful though he was, it did not seem as if he was going to put up any more resistance.

They drove back into the square. The villager climbed out—for the moment he was too dispirited to try running away. It was obvious he was numbed to see the terrible destruction up close.

Mulanda started questioning the man. But all he received was a bitter reply.

"He wants to know why we did this to his village."

"Tell him we didn't," said Bolan, "and we're just as interested as he is in whoever's responsible."

Mulanda translated and exchanged several more comments as the brawny Nabu tribesman gestured to the southwest.

"He was with the other men of the village. They hid the few cattle and goats they've got in the hills over there. He was out hunting a lion that's been raiding their livestock."

The native spoke in quick, jerky phrases, holding up three fingers in front of Mulanda before making the same sign for Bolan's benefit. The tracker continued to translate simultaneously. "This morning—maybe two hours ago—he saw three truckloads of foreign soldiers. They were miles from any of the tracks, where no white man goes. Ziemba, that's his name, took a shortcut through the hill country...to warn the village. He ran most of the way...."

"He must have seen Scarr," said Katz.

"Ask him which way these soldiers were heading."

Ziemba made a zigzag motion toward the north.

"He wasn't sure where they could be heading— there's only a desert in front of them," explained the Mussengamba. "That's why he came back to warn his neighbors—just in case the foreigners decided to pay them a visit."

"It tells us two things," said Bolan. "First, that Yagoda and Scarr are traveling by day. And, second,

that this butchery couldn't have been their handi-
work.''

"Then who in bloody hell did this?" asked McCarter.

"Mumungo!" Rawson's reply was loud and harsh.
He turned away from the doorway of one of the
burned-out *rondevals* and advanced stiffly on the
small group in the center of the square. He was holding something behind one of his trouser legs.

"General Mumungo?" The Englishman was puzzled. It didn't make sense.

"He was only a sergeant before he got some big
ideas." Rawson's laugh was a short, cynical bark.
"I'm not saying he was here personally, but his men
were. They did this."

"Are you certain?" Bolan challenged him.

Rawson nodded as he stopped in front of the
others, then with a dramatic flourish he produced the
object he had been holding out of sight. It appeared
to be a long hard whip, but it was covered with a gray
film of ash. "Do you know what this is?"

Bolan was impatient to get on the trail of Yagoda's
unit. There was no time to play games.

"Well, do you?" repeated Rawson.

The American shook his head.

"It's a penis!"

The Phoenix men stared in disbelief. Even Ohara
looked down from his sentry post to inspect what
Rawson was holding up for display.

"Hippo maybe . . . or buffalo."

"A *sjambok*?" guessed Katz, half-remembering
some mercenary gossip in a nameless bar.

"That's what they call it in South Africa," agreed the leathery-faced surveyor. "Up here, it's known as a *fimbo*. They cut off the penis, stretch it and dry it hard...."

"And it makes an unusual kind of whip," Bolan concluded grimly.

"But very effective as you can see." Rawson used the *fimbo* to point to the body Bolan had cut down. "He was beaten to death with this. It's the mark of Mumungo's personal bodyguards, the Leopard Patrol."

Mulanda had been making a whispered translation for the villager. Ziemba uttered an angry curse. For the first time since Bolan had tackled him, Ziemba stood fully erect, his dark eyes glittering above the pitted tracks of his tribal scars. His face was a primal mask of vengeance.

Ohara suddenly straightened and pointed over the collapsed roof of a *rondeval* toward the open ground beyond the village. "Hey, over there...."

"Looks like the rest of the villagers coming back," grunted Kambolo, shielding his eyes from the midday sun.

An irregular row of barbed bushes had concealed the sandy ravine where the other women, children and three old men had been hiding for the past couple of hours. One of the village elders limped forward, still uncertain of what to make of the foreign intruders although reassured to see Ziemba had not been harmed by them.

Katz shook his head sadly. These people lived all their lives in fear—fear of marauding lions and mercenaries, of starvation and cruelly ambitious tyrants. And yet, somehow, they hung on to their tattered, stubborn pride despite it all. The unlucky ones who had been caught in the village by the Leopard Patrol had been tortured to death rather than reveal where the animals or their neighbors were hidden.

"Mumungo must be desperate for taxes to have sent out his own crack troopers," Rawson said to Bolan.

"They're on a tax-gathering patrol? Yes, it makes sense. Mumungo will be desperate to raise the funds to pay off the army he's drafted to defend himself."

"Colonel Phoenix." Mulanda caught Bolan's attention with this formal address. "Ziemba asks if he may accompany us. He has vowed to make these murderers pay—that's his own brother lying there."

"Ours is a different battle," replied Bolan. "We cannot help these people. And he can't come with us."

He turned away and signaled for the others to climb back aboard the truck. They must waste no more precious time here. They had to get on the trail of Yagoda's gang immediately or risk losing them in the forbidding desert that still lay ahead. He could not allow himself to be sidetracked into tangling with Mumungo's Leopard Patrol.

"Move it, McCarter, load up!" ordered Katz. "Let's get Scarr and then get the hell out of here!"

BOLAN CONTROLLED THE ANGER he felt welling up inside as the Land Rover bucked and slithered along the rutted track that wound north. He had seen it in the eyes of Manning and the Englishman. Ohara and Encizo revealed little, but he knew they felt it too. They would all like the chance to get even with Mumungo's murderous bullies. But the Phoenix team could not be diverted from its primary objective. Bolan was not a man to run from a fight, but right now he could only hope that the Leopard Patrol would not come between them and the Angolan unit.

"Where was Mumungo's mob heading for?" he asked their guide.

"The tracks led to the south toward Shogololo," Rawson replied. "But that doesn't mean a damn thing. They won't stick to the road, otherwise all the villages down that way would be alerted, giving the villagers a chance to hide whatever money, grain, or cattle they have. No, the Leopard men will crisscross through the bush, strike anywhere without warning. That way the drum talk can't raise an alarm."

"So we could run into them even on this trail?" asked Manning.

"Let's hope not! But we'd best keep our eyes peeled," advised the South African.

The group remained silent for a minute, then Bolan asked, "What was it like under Bambabele?"

"Some of his officials were idealistic, others were corrupt. The bureaucracy moved slowly, but it moved." The surveyor shrugged. "And you couldn't make head or tail of his foreign policy. I guess it was much like any other infant nation taking its first steps."

Katz was right, Bolan conceded to himself. To help

put Bambabele back into power would be a favor to these people. And to do that they first had to snatch the diamonds and the papers from Scarr.

"Come on, Kambolo, can't you make this crate go a little faster?" urged Rawson, sensing the commander's impatience.

"Sounds like you do believe in the treasure after all," remarked Bolan.

"There must be something to the rumors," the other man confessed. "It's the only thing that could have saved Scarr from being stopped by the Angolans." He pointed to the long, dark thunderheads strung out low along the horizon. "It looks like the rains are coming at last. I've got a float plane waiting for you at Baruka and you won't be able to take off if a storm's pissing down. We have to reach it before that lot catches up with us."

Bolan twisted around to observe the cloud bank. The truck was keeping up with them, but it was uncomfortable for the men bouncing around in the back.

"How far to the desert?" asked Manning.

"About an hour," said Rawson. "Don't worry, we'll catch up with Scarr's people on the Devil's Forge. They'll have to stick to the track to make sure they hit the wells. But Mulanda back there, he knows all the ways across the Forge. Used to track down renegade Bushmen through that country. He'll find us a shortcut and we'll be right on their tail."

"And we'll just have to sit there until they lead us to the cache," said Bolan. His one aim now was to catch up with Scarr's gang. The gathering storm clouds only emphasized their race against time.

"Hey, pull up!" shouted Manning. "Something's wrong...."

They all looked back down the track. The truck had slewed to one side. It was sagging badly to the left.

Bolan cursed beneath his breath.

## 8

*"Merde!"* grunted Katz as he stepped down onto the track. He knew it—this whole mission was jinxed.

McCarter surveyed the monotonous expanse of stunted brush stretching away to the brown and purple wall of the Mambosso hills. "Not much chance of the AA coming along, is there?"

The older man gave him a blank stare.

"The Automobile Association," explained McCarter.

Katz merely grunted as he bent down to see what had gone wrong. He was not in the mood for McCarter's humor. Manning climbed out with a puzzled frown.

"How bad is it?" shouted Bolan, as the Land Rover backed up the narrow trail.

"The shock's gone...damn, looks like the whole mounting's been torn out!"

Manning shook his head regretfully. He should have checked over the truck back in that Nabu village; but a quick maintenance inspection could not have prevented the damage. He had to admit it, the colonel had been setting a reckless pace.

Bolan turned to Rawson. "How far is the nearest village?"

The surveyor looked to Mulanda for an answer.
"Four, maybe five miles."

"Have you got a tow rope?" inquired Bolan.

Rawson nodded.

"Get it!" Bolan ordered crisply. He was not going
to lose their momentum.

Kambolo and Mulanda pulled out the wire cable
from the truck and hitched it to the back of the jeep.

"We'll tow the truck into the next village and fix it
there." Bolan paused just long enough to glance at
the distant hills. Had Yagoda reached that far already? Was Scarr guiding the Angolans down onto
the desert plain beyond? He knew they were close.
And they were not going to slip away from him now.

THE BALUBA VILLAGE appeared to be marginally more
prosperous than the Nabu settlement. Two rows of
solid square huts were laid out along the east-west
axis of the wide clearing that served as its only thor-
oughfare. The smoke hovering in the air was innocent gray wraiths from their cooking fires.

A well-developed young girl, bare from the waist
up, was loading sacks with manioc flour under the
shade of a thatched lean-to. She stopped singing and
straightened up as the Land Rover towed the listing
truck down the village street. She made no attempt to
cover herself from these strangers.

McCarter pursed his lips in a silent whistle of
admiration. Katz noticed his reaction but said nothing. This team was too well trained to start the kind
of trouble he had once had to deal with in this country.

"No harm in looking, eh?" said the Englishman. "She's a real beauty!"

"So long as it's just looking," cautioned Katz.

A child watched their approach wide-eyed with curiosity from the entrance of a hut, then turned and ran back inside.

Manning cradled his rifle, wondering how many unseen eyes were following their procession as it limped through the town.

Mulanda knew this place. The blacksmith had a small charcoal forge at the far end of the street.

His workshop was three low mud walls and four sturdy corner posts supporting a roof of matted twigs. A tattered portrait poster of Buka Ntanga stared from one of the uprights; judging from the stains that were sprayed across the crinkled paper, Bolan guessed his image was spat at more than it was ever revered.

They should be safe enough for the time it took to repair the truck. Time! That was the problem. If they weren't close on the heels of Yagoda's unit when they finished the desert crossing, they might lose them completely in those overgrown uplands.

The blacksmith was a beefy fellow, with tribal scars decorating the blue black skin above his temples. Bits and pieces of his work lay scattered round the entrance to his forge. His chief business was hammering out arrowheads and spearpoints, and repairing the tribesmen's ancient long-barreled rifles.

Mulanda explained the situation. The blacksmith nodded gravely but clearly he had no understanding of what was required.

"This is no bloody good," Rawson muttered angrily. "Mulanda, tell him we'll pay him well, but I need to use his tools. I'll do the bloody job myself!"

Kambolo unhitched the truck on Katz's orders, then drove Ohara and McCarter back in the Land Rover to stand watch at the opposite end of town. Manning and Rawson stripped off their shirts and set to work as the blacksmith began pumping the leather bellows.

When Kambolo returned, Bolan took twenty paces down the street to look at the fetish shrine that had caught his eye. Four tall sticks marked the corners of the sacred rectangle, inside which a smaller square was marked with feathers and bits of bone. Lying in the very center was a broken spearhead.

"What does it mean?" Bolan asked Kambolo, but the citified black could only shrug. He stood there toying with his cigarette lighter.

"It is to keep away evil," explained Mulanda. "To ward off the spirits that stalk the land at night."

"Like the Leopard men who come to collect the taxes?"

Mulanda nodded.

Bolan crouched, resting against the mud wall, as the glimmer of an idea began to form.

"We're in trouble," confessed Manning. "It's going to take at least three or four hours to fix it securely."

Bolan did not question Gary's estimate. He knew the Canadian engineer would do his best.

Manning looked toward the hills. "If only there was some way we could stop them."

"We don't want to stop them," Katz contradicted him. "Not yet. Not until they've led us to Scarr's hiding place. Then we'll stop them dead. No, what we need is a way to slow them down."

"Like a Bushmen's raid," said Bolan, slowly getting to his feet. "Mulanda!"

"Yes, baas."

"Mr. Rawson tells me you know the desert well."

"I've crossed it many times. I know the shortcuts, the quicksands...."

"You used to track men down there?"

"Sometimes raiding parties would try to hide out there," Mulanda replied, nodding.

"This time you're going to guide a raiding party!" Mulanda smiled.

"Could you overtake those other trucks before they reached the water hole?"

"Yes, if we leave now."

Bolan turned to the others. "They can't reach those wells till after dark. That's where I'm going to hit them. No guns. Just knives and spears. We'll do enough damage to slow them down."

"Without tipping them off that they're being followed by an armed patrol. Brilliant!" said Katz. It would buy them the time they so desperately needed.

"Gary, I want you and Rawson to repair that truck quickly. Yakov, you and McCarter are to stand guard. I'm taking Rafael, Keio and Mulanda with me."

"As soon as we can roll, we'll follow the main track across the Forge," Katz said.

"No. Even if you're finished sooner, wait until

first light before setting off. We can't take any more risks with that truck," instructed Bolan. "We'll make our way back along the track and hook up with you. I'll make sure Yagoda is slowed down. They won't get far. Mulanda, collect some of those spears. And give the man some money. We won't be bringing them back."

THE LAND ROVER blazed a smoking trail across the wasted landscape.

A broken notch in the steep wall of the Mambosso hills indicated where the pass lay in front of them, but for a while the faded gray brown cliffs hovered on a shimmering heat haze and seemed to draw no closer.

Bolan half turned and saw the heavy brows above Encizo's square face furrowed in somber reflection.

"I was thinking about that man back there," he admitted, his voice thick with feeling, "whipped to death! What did he call it? A *fimbo*?"

Mulanda nodded, amused by the foreigners' revulsion.

Ohara's face remained inscrutable. At that moment Bolan realized that the roots of violence in this ancient land stretched back to the primeval past, when man was born of the killer ape. This soil might be parched for water, but it was steeped in blood from the very dawn of time.

Mulanda began to slow down. Bolan fired a glance across at him.

"The railroad's just ahead," explained the driver.

Two dull ribbons of corroded steel followed the

contours of the last flat ledge before the jagged barrier of the Mambosso range.

"To the west, it goes down to the towns along the upper Kasai," the tracker said, flicking his fingers to the left. "To the east, this line curves around the desert and connects with a network of old tracks that served the mines. Not used much anymore."

Mulanda brought the vehicle to a halt and sat looking at the trail on the far side of the rails.

"What's the matter now?"

"See them, baas? Fresh tracks—two or three trucks, I'd say."

Bolan stood up and saw the impressions left in the dirt by Yagoda's unit. But how fresh were they?

"Can you catch them?"

"Sure," replied Mulanda as he trod on the accelerator.

On the far side of the pass the road dropped swiftly through a twisting series of hairpin curves. Although the Mambosso hills cut off the plain beyond from the cooling breezes and healing rain, they offered no shade from the pitiless sun. It hovered over them now, a molten copper disk suspended in the sky.

The desert started innocuously enough. There was even a small stand of stunted fever trees at the bottom of the hill, but their skeletal branches served only as a roost for a watchful secretary bird.

A solitary termite hill marked the beginning of the sandy plain. Encizo glanced out at the bleached remains of some long-dead creature that lay half-covered by drifting sand. As far as the eye could see, uneven heaps of brown- and black-streaked rocks studded the rust-colored soil. The Devil's Forge was aptly named; it was as if someone had raked out the cinders of Hell and dumped them here. And this terrain was as harsh as the feeling in Bolan's heart.

Those few odd patches where the dirt was softer still carried the imprint of Yagoda's vehicles. Occasionally Bolan would sweep the way ahead through his field glasses. The intruders could not be that far in front, not at the speed Mulanda was driving.

Bolan had no illusions that helping restore Bambabele to power would mean the people of Kuranda could enjoy the freedoms of a Western-style democracy, but at least he was going to make Yagoda wish he had never strayed so far from Moscow.

"Hold on!" Mulanda called out. "Here's where we turn off."

The main track curved away in a bulging loop toward the northwest to detour around a treacherous patch of quicksand. Without hesitation, the guide spun the wheel over and plunged down a tortuous ravine scarcely wide enough for the Land Rover to pass through safely. It was certainly too narrow for the East German trucks Yagoda was using, even if Scarr knew this shortcut, which Bolan seriously doubted.

"How far to the wells?"

"Maybe two hours, maybe less," grunted the driver, not taking his eyes from the sloping path. "At least three by the track. We'll beat them, baas!"

The men hung on in silence as Mulanda hit the bottom of the wadi, shifted gears, and accelerated along the dry riverbed. It had been years since sufficient rainfall had spilled over the Mambosso range to fill these ancient watercourses. They had become lifeless arteries cracking the sun-hammered surface of the Forge.

Nothing, it seemed, could survive out here.

But somehow it did.

A black-backed jackal and its mate lay panting in the shadows of an abandoned burrow. Their long ears twitched cautiously as they suffered the worst of the late-afternoon heat.

And a leopard slinked softly toward the desert's only watering place. The great spotted cat was tired and frustrated. She had been chased from her territory by a younger female. That morning she'd been outrun in the foothills by a klipspringer that had leaped up the sheer ledges and proved as cunning as it was nimble in eluding pursuit. Cheated of its best hope for a meal in days, the angry predator now padded hungrily toward the water hole and its last chance for a kill. . . .

"THERE IT IS." Mulanda pointed through the grime-caked windshield. "I call it Pyramid Hill. Shoba Well lies less than half a mile beyond it."

Bolan checked the map lying on his knee—the well was the only feature marked in the midst of this desolation.

He twisted his wrist and glanced at his watch. The black driver was pleased that the big American gave him such an approving nod. "One hour, fifty minutes—you did a good job, Mulanda."

"It'll be dark soon. I think we get here just in time."

"Okay, we'll leave the rifles here," Bolan told the others.

They hid the Land Rover in a shallow depression behind the hill and proceeded to the crest on foot.

Ohara was glad to get out and stretch his long legs after the spine-jolting ride. The thin scattering of oddly shaped boulders around the slopes of Pyramid Hill afforded them cover to do a recon of the land.

It was not necessary for the guide to point out the location of Shoba Well. About six hundred yards from where they lay, a large fissure in the rock provided a natural cistern that was constantly replenished by a mineral-rich spring. The few bushes and a fringe of tough grasses that ringed the wall were the only signs of greenery they had seen all afternoon.

They were looking almost directly into the setting sun, but Ohara's sharp eyes could make out movements around the life-giving pool.

"Not men." Mulanda shook his head. "No, they are creatures of the desert. They come for their evening drink."

"All we can do now is watch and wait," Bolan said. "Try to get a little rest. You've all got a spear and a knife?"

They each nodded, but Ohara asked, "Are you sure they're going to stop here?"

"They've had an even longer drive across the desert than we did. I'm confident they'll rest here for a while."

"After all, where could be safer?" Encizo grinned at the irony of his own remark.

"Yagoda and Scarr have got to figure they'll be secure out here in the middle of nowhere," agreed Bolan. "Remember, when we move in we want them to think it was the work of Bushmen. So no fancy tricks. Just grab what weapons you can, slash some tires, steal their food...."

"What about the men?" Ohara asked, running his thumb along the well-honed blade.

"Use your handguns only if you're absolutely forced to. Hit and run! Rendezvous at the vehicle... and we're away. That ravine back there should muffle the noise of our engine."

Mulanda tapped the commander's shoulder and jabbed his finger at the faint dust haze in the distance.

"Okay, this is it," said Bolan, "spread out and take cover."

Ohara melted behind a boulder about ten feet away. Encizo and the tracker lay down in a gully just below Bolan's position.

The next move was up to Yagoda.

The small animals drinking by the pool scampered away at the drone of the approaching engines. In the brief transition of twilight, the three Star trucks pulled up in formation on the gravel pan beside the track. Bolan watched through his binoculars as the men piled out—it was his first chance to view the enemy.

There were eight men in each vehicle, plus the driver and a guy in the passenger seat: thirty soldiers in all. They were uniformly garbed in jungle-camouflage fatigues. And, unless there were an unusual number of black Cubans mixed in, the team seemed evenly divided between Angolan troops and Castro's mercenaries.

Bolan slowly panned the milling group below. Suddenly he stopped, moving the binoculars back an inch or two to focus on two men taller than the others, one checking his map case, the other talking and pointing to the north. Probably Scarr and the Russian discussing their situation.

Even in the failing light, Bolan could make out the Afrikaaner with his reddish gold hair. He was wearing a sweat-stained bush shirt that looked two sizes too large. The diet in Quita prison was not calculated to put on weight. Yagoda listened carefully, then issued his own instructions to the Cuban sergeant. The man from Moscow was calling the shots.

Sentries were posted near the trucks and at the four corners of a perimeter line. One of the guards was facing the hill, but it was too gloomy now for him to make out much more than a dark silhouette against the spangled backdrop of the African night. Other men were detailed to light a fire and brew up.

The rest of the platoon flopped on the ground and waited for the rations to be distributed. Some were smoking and a couple of them just flaked out for a nap. It had been an exhausting ride.

Curses, laughter and orders in Spanish drifted up the hillside. Encizo gripped his spear more tightly. He knew precisely why the colonel had picked him for this nightprobe. It was a tactical decision.

Rafael Encizo, survivor of the Bay of Pigs invasion, was a Cuban patriot. He spoke the same language as some of the men standing watch down there. But it was the only thing left that he had in common with them. Fidel Castro had mortgaged his beloved island to the Kremlin. But tonight—in a place so far away from the lush Caribbean—he had another chance to work toward evening the score.

Rafael Encizo had not chosen this killing ground. Those troops down at the well had come here before him—men who allowed themselves to be used as the whores of an alien ideology.

Soon it would be time to strike. He waited for Phoenix to give the signal.

THE SCENT WAS CARRIED on the sluggish night air. The wary cat froze in midstride at the base of the hill and listened and sniffed again. It was the unmistakable smell of danger: man smell!

If the leopard had not been so hungry she would have retreated, but she needed meat, any meat. Head low and jaw open, the big carnivore stalked silently through the rocks to the crown of the hill.

Tonight she would eat....

9

David McCarter casually strolled along the village street, the FLN balanced lightly on his shoulder.

"Evening!" He touched the soft brim of his jungle hat as he greeted the old lady who was smoking a clay pipe in the doorway of her hut. She gave him a gap-toothed smile in return.

The girl they had seen grinding flour turned away and vanished before he could address her. McCarter shrugged—she certainly was a looker! He saw the shadowy figure of Katz circling past the end of the street. "Yakov! It's just about time for me to spell you. Anything happening?"

"No, it's as quiet as the grave. Have they finished fixing the truck?"

"I think Gary's about through with it. Seems to have been a bitch of a job."

"I'm sure he's done the best he can. But I cannot tell whether Rawson is more of a hindrance or a help...."

McCarter screwed up his nose in obvious distaste.

"Watch out when you patrol past those acacia trees," Katz cautioned him. "There's a narrow gully running right along behind the huts over there. I almost fell into it in the dark."

"Thanks for the warning." McCarter sauntered away, but then turned. "You watch out for Kambolo's curried chicken—at least, that's what he claims it is. If this were the Savoy I'd have sent it back to the chef."

The older man smiled. McCarter might play the clown at times, but he was as good as they came—which was a lot more than he was willing to say for their guide.

Rawson was already tackling his second plate of Kambolo's dubious cuisine when Katz got back to the forge. Gary Manning was trying to wash himself off in a rusted oil drum half-full of stagnant water. After the long afternoon's struggle to repair the truck with the blacksmith's inadequate tools, the two men did not appear to be on speaking terms.

As Katz helped himself to a deliberately small serving of the chicken concoction, Rawson watched closely to see how the Israeli would manage with his artificial hand. Finally, curiosity got the better of him. "Did you lose it in the fighting down here?"

"No. In the Six Day War."

"Must have been a tough break."

A wistful look crossed Katz's face as he thought of his only son who had died in the same antipersonnel-mine blast that had ripped away his arm.

He shrugged—his personal contribution to his country's victory was small enough when compared to the sacrifice others had been called upon to make. Then he spoke.

"What about you, Mr. Rawson? Where do you come from?"

"Jo'burg, originally. Came up here on a three-year contract—nearly twenty years ago. Too late for me to go back now."

"And you've worked for Afric Ore all that time?"

"For one INGOT division or another, yes. Surveying, track laying, supervising mining operations. . . you name it, I've done it. Sure I've compromised, but then we all have to at some time or other, don't we?"

Katz seemed to nod in agreement, but the tilt of his head was quite perfunctory—compromise was not something he was familiar with. "You stayed on after the coup. What happened?"

"At the time, I didn't know any more about it than Bambabele himself. He was out of the country at an All-African Economic Summit when Mumungo grabbed power. And I was up in the bush—in fact, it was near where we're heading for—I was trying to get a derailed train back on the tracks.

"Got back to the city to find Kuranda had a new leader. That's the way it happens in these countries. The shift of power is swift. Here today, gone tomorrow. But I stayed on—somebody had to look after things. You know, those bastards haven't given me a raise in five years. That's gratitude for you!"

"You ever had any trouble with Mumungo's men before?"

Manning, who had joined the group after his clean up, looked interested in Rawson's answer, but not enough to join in the conversation.

"Not personally. But I've seen enough of it. Like this morning. They're mean bastards, the Leopard

Patrol. Well named, too—the leopard is the most vicious and dangerous wild animal in Africa. Personally, I wouldn't want to run into either, men or beasts...."

Rawson had a few questions of his own. While Katz leaned back against the mud wall and chewed on his supper, the surveyor took the initiative. "Why doesn't your boss set up an ambush for Scarr's mob in the desert? It would be a good place to catch them on the way back from Blood River."

"I suppose there's a chance they might try a different route out," Katz told him. "Anyway, who can tell what'll happen up in the high country? Once Scarr has led them to the cache, his usefulness is expended."

"I'm sure he was the first to figure that out," added Manning.

"So he might try anything to stay alive. No, Mr. Rawson, we've got to hit them just as soon as they've recovered the loot. The timing is critical."

"Your only worry is to get us out," the Canadian said to Rawson. There was a thinly veiled threat in his words.

"I've got one of the old company float planes waiting for us at Baruka. It's a small lake about forty miles northwest of here." Rawson returned Manning's stare quite evenly. "I'll get you out."

Rawson tossed the remains of his supper in the dirt. "I think I'll turn in," said their guide, not inquiring if he might take a turn standing watch. He belched and hurried away to fetch his bedroll from the back of the truck.

"Are you sure it'll get us the rest of the way?" Katz asked the engineer, once Rawson was out of earshot. It was an unfair question and he knew it even as he spoke.

"I've done what I can," replied Manning. "We'll see in the morning. I'm going to get my head down, too."

Katz sat alone in the darkness, smoking a last cigarette. Sitting in the soft glow of an oil lantern, he observed how pitch-black it looked out there. Colonel Phoenix was right. It would be crazy to risk pushing on through the night.

He still couldn't put his finger on precisely what it was that nagged at him. Was it Rawson? If he had no particular company loyalty or political conviction, then what the hell was he doing here? Was it the bad luck they had had with their transportation? Or was it just Africa?

He knew it would be a long night, waiting for the others to get back.

THE FIRES HAD BURNED LOW. The sentries had been changed after supper. And the men were now bedded down. It was still early but there was nothing else to do but sleep, for Yagoda would surely have them up before dawn.

Bolan decided to wait another couple of minutes before issuing his final orders. Encizo would take the point. He and Ohara would be close behind. Mulanda would watch the left flank.

Physically, mentally, Bolan prepared himself. It was time for The Executioner to take his nightwalk.

The men asleep at Shoba Well did not know how close Death would brush past them this night. But for the lucky ones it would be only a temporary reprieve. None would escape the appointment they must keep on Blood River.

Every sense was now alert...and some survival instinct far below the level of consciousness compelled Bolan to turn. The alarm bells were screaming in his brain as he whirled to face the ridge behind.

He was half sitting, his back to the boulder, when the hungry cat sprang...one hundred twenty pounds of whipcord sinew, taut muscle and slashing fangs smashed into him.

The spear was knocked from his hand. There was no time to scramble for the weapon in the split second he had to defend himself.

*Panthera pardus* is one of the most efficient killing machines ever evolved by nature. But, like all the big cats, it has one structural deficiency: no collarbone! As Bolan struggled to one side, the leopard twisted the other way and Bolan was able to loop his arms under her powerful forelimbs. Exerting every ounce of strength, he splayed open her legs and began pulling them back against her neck. The cat snarled viciously as she felt her shoulders begin to dislocate under the relentless pressure.

Mulanda crouched wide-eyed and immobile, transfixed by the struggle of man against wild beast. Encizo felt helpless. Any light, any sound, any further action on their part would give them all away.

Although the sharp hind claws had raked his leg in

the first attack, Bolan did not cry out—not even for help from his comrades.

His whole being, body and soul, was focused on the defeat of the writhing, snarling man-eater. It was those claws he must avoid. With a lightning-fast maneuver, Bolan managed to straddle the great cat. Crushing her pelvis in a scissors grip, Bolan hooked his own legs between the beast's and levered them open.

Ohara dared not jab out blindly with his spear. He might wound the colonel. With unerring accuracy, he threw his heavy knife into the ground about a foot away from the struggling pair.

With its front paws still clawing wildly at the air, Bolan could not relax his grip on the creature for one moment. It writhed and twisted, snarling, trying to shake off the heavy weight of its intended victim. Still Bolan clung for his life.

He managed to keep the predator's head tucked forward with the choke hold, but he could still feel its fetid breath as it gave a low grunting cough.

Each agonizing second lasted an eternity. The hungry leopard found some hidden reserve of desperate strength and began to squirm out from under him.

It was now or.... Bolan snatched the knife up faster than a striking snake. The leopard twisted about, ready for its revenge, but it was too late. Ten inches of razor-sharp steel sliced through its rib cage, and the tip of the blade cut through its aorta.

Seizing the creature by the throat, Bolan rammed home the point a second time, and this thrust skewered its heart. A crimson flood gushed back along the blood run in warm, heavy spurts. The cat fell on its side, shuddered and lay still.

The nightmare struggle was over.

Ohara was the first one to wriggle forward. The naturally rank smell of the cat now mingled with the hot stench of its lifeblood still puddling in the dirt.

"Are you hurt?" he whispered urgently.

"No, not badly," replied Bolan. He was still trying to catch his breath. "Are they on the alert?"

The tall Japanese peered round the side of the boulder. The sudden flare of a match lit up two faces as they poked their cigarettes in the flame. A couple of the guards had heard the sounds. "They probably think it's a hunting animal on the prowl."

"That's all it was." Bolan shook his head. It was terrible to be forced to kill such a magnificent creature. "There's no way they'll risk coming up here in the darkness to investigate it."

Mulanda looked down at the body of the cat. It was more than five feet long. His friends would never believe him. He could hardly believe it himself: he had seen a man take on a full-grown leopard and win. This American warrior truly was The Powerful One.

"Bwana Mukubwa!" he breathed, his head lowered in respect. Gone was his slightly sarcastic "baas"—now it was "Great Master!"

"Rafael, you lead. Keio and I will be right behind you. Mulanda, move out to the left." This was no time for hero worship. "Let's go. We've got some hunting of our own to do!"

THE MOON was barely more than a discarded fingernail among the myriad stars that twinkled over the African plain, but the midnight sky was bright enough for Encizo to pick out the solitary sentry hunched in the bushes to his right.

His frogman training stood him in good stead, even here—whether landing at night on a Caribbean beachhead or creeping across the sands around a water hole in Africa, the Cuban could move as silently as a sidewinder. And he was every bit as deadly. Yagoda's watchdog was in for a surprise.

Encizo moved swiftly past the picket, turned and straightened up. Now he sauntered toward the guard from the one direction the guy was not expecting trouble.

Still the man turned. *"¿Quién . . . ?"*

*"Tomas. Está bien,"* Rafael quickly reassured him. One of the squad had to be named Tomas. *"¿Qué hora es?"*

The guard checked the luminous dial of his watch. *"Son las doce y cuarto. ¿Qué pasa?"*

Encizo stepped closer, apparently fiddling with his fly. It was obvious to the sentry what "Tomas" was about to do.

Satisfied, the sentry turned away with a chuckle. He was still grinning when Encizo's hand clamped around his mouth. From left to right, the razor edge of the knife sank deep, through skin, muscle and gristle, to open up another wider, bloodwet grin . . . it slashed through everything vital. There was only a soft gurgling sound as Encizo gently lowered the corpse of his ex-compatriot to the ground.

Bolan and Ohara hurried through the unguarded gap in the perimeter. They could see the dark shape of the Cuban nightfighter crouchwalking across the open patch in front of them. Ohara veered off to the right, toward the bundled forms of the sleeping soldiers. Bolan followed fast on Encizo's heels.

Over on the far side, the Angolan guard was pacing nervously back and forth, AK-47 held ready, still wondering what dreadful creature was prowling out there on its nightly hunt. He never saw Mulanda. The assegai flashed out of the darkness, split the sentry's sternum and erupted from his back.

He swayed for a moment, then fell to his knees grasping the decorated shaft, too surprised to even call out. Before he could summon the last of his strength to shout a warning, the Mussengamba tracker was upon him. A blade glittered cold in the starlight as the fallen man's throat, too, was slit from side to side.

Mulanda picked up the AK-47 out of the grass. In his opinion not much of a weapon, but for booty it was all right.

Keio Ohara, the man who had forgotten more than a *ninja* was ever taught, found what he was looking for—Colonel Boris Yagoda. The youthful KGB officer was wrapped tight inside a poncho. But he was not to be the shadow warrior's target. Keio wanted the man lying right beside him: the Cuban sergeant.

The fellow turned restlessly, emitted a snuffling little snore, and murmured, *"Te quiero..."*; whoever he was making this sleepy declaration of love to would never hear him say it again.

Keio worked swiftly, silently and utterly without mercy. What he did was not pretty. It was not intended to be. And when he had finished the grisly task, Ohara left the hefty blade sticking through the sergeant's chest, then he melted back into the night.

Encizo punctured one of the tires with his bloodstained blade and turned to slash at the wheel on the next truck. A sentry appeared behind him without warning, wondering what the hell was going on. He thought one of his buddies was on the prowl for extra rations.

"Hey!" was all he got out before Bolan rammed a spear through his shoulder blade. Encizo, his heart still pounding from surprise, reached up and caught both man and rifle before they could clatter on the gravel.

"How are you doing?" hissed Bolan.

Encizo nodded. He was just about through.

"Grab some ammo or food from the back of that other truck and let's get the hell out of here!"

"You got it."

Bolan swung a sack of rice over his shoulder and began to withdraw. He was limping slightly; the cat's claws had dug deep.

But he was not as badly mauled as Yagoda's platoon.

In single file they scrambled round the side of the hill. Ohara carried a box of grenades. Mulanda had the rifle slung over his shoulder and both arms wrapped round a large carton of canned goods. Encizo was lugging two metal containers of 7.62mm ammunition.

They crowded into the Land Rover with the rewards of their night raid. Keio handed Bolan a medical pack. He ripped open his tattered trouser leg, doused the cuts with disinfectant, dusted the wound with powder and tied on a dressing. It was the best he could do as Mulanda rolled forward and followed the wadi without revving the engine.

No shouts of surprise or alarm echoed after them.

## 10

Katz propped himself on one elbow and shook his head to clear it. It was later than he intended to wake. Dawn was filtering through a bank of gray clouds to the east. It would be fully light in minutes. McCarter was still asleep just inside the doorway to the forge.

Katz splashed some water over his face. Manning must have been patrolling the outskirts of the village. Maybe Rawson was with him—there was no sign of the surveyor.

The villagers were already starting about their day's business. They kept to the rhythms of the sun and the seasons. The blacksmith plodded down the street carrying a basket of charcoal and dried cattle dung for his fire.

Katz was getting his gear together when the first scream shattered the early-morning stillness.

A second angry, protesting cry came as Katz raced down the dirt road, Uzi at the ready.

Rawson had the girl pinned down in the dust beside her hut. The cotton blouse she'd put on was ripped open. One callused hand was grasping her breast, the other was trying to shut up her screams. She squirmed to free herself but was pinned down by Rawson's weight as he straddled her middle.

"You bloody fool, Rawson!" Katz held the SMG waist high and pointing at the surveyor. Manning sprinted in from the other direction to investigate the shouts. "Do you want to screw everything up? Get off her. Now!"

The girl lay absolutely still. McCarter appeared at Katz's shoulder. But Rawson remained where he was, weighing his chances. They wouldn't dare shoot him. They needed him.

"You've got till I count to three," warned the Israeli. "If you don't move, you're a dead man."

The icy tone in his voice left no room for bargaining. "One."

Rawson knew it was hopeless to even think of going for the pistol at his hip. The three Phoenix men had their weapons trained directly on him. He would be cut to shreds before his gun cleared the holster.

"Two."

McCarter's finger began to tighten on the trigger. He saw something flicker in Rawson's eyes. Fear... hope?

"Three." It wasn't Katz who spoke. The deep voice came from behind them. "And now I suggest you all drop your guns!"

Their heads jerked around. The black officer standing in the street wore leopard-spot dungarees and a camouflage *kepi* pulled menacingly low over his eyes, which were shielded behind aviator-styled sunglasses. He waved the muzzle of his pistol toward the ground. "I said throw down your weapons!"

Three other Leopard Patrol troopers were spread out behind him. Their rifles were leveled and ready to fire. If they were surprised to find foreign mercenaries in this out-of-the-way village it didn't show. They waited only for the order to cut down these uninvited guests.

Katz dropped the Uzi. It was the only thing he could do to buy time. He cursed himself for having been taken unawares. Dawn was the obvious time for the Leopard Patrol to strike. He cursed Rawson for causing the commotion that had diverted his attention.

Manning felt the bile rise at the back of his throat as he let go of the Belgian rifle. It toppled into the dust. He was the one who was supposed to have been on watch!

Rawson did not know whether to laugh or cry. He had literally been caught with his pants down. He was not going to lose face over the girl now... but that was scant relief. He just might lose his life. The Leopard Patrol was not known for its tender mercies.

"And your side arms, too! Very slowly!"

Captain Mwekango, the officer with the sunglasses, was enjoying himself. The early morning hours were always the best time to surprise a village, but he had not counted on a catch like this! He nodded to the NCO who, in turn, signaled down the street for their truck to move in.

With the mercs disarmed, Mwekango's men relaxed a little—not their trigger fingers, just their expressions. These four were big men—three of them were—but without their guns they didn't look like *les Affreux*.

Mwekango was very curious about what this small

unit was doing in Kuranda. It was going to be an amusing morning's work finding out. He could smell a promotion.

"Take them down to that blacksmith's forge," he ordered, as more of his men jumped out of the truck. "And stoke up the fire!"

"SLOW DOWN." Bolan spoke to his driver.

Mulanda eased his foot off the gas pedal.

Protected by an undulating ridge of granite, they had rejoined the main track about seven miles south of Shoba Well. Driving through the dark had made the return journey almost twice as long. There had been no junctions or intersections with any other road and yet they had seen no sign of their comrades.

Bolan glanced at his watch for the fourth time in half an hour. Surely there was no way they could have missed them?

The sun had broken through the clouds as they climbed the steep, twisting pass through the Mambosso hills.

"They must have got at least this far," said Encizo.

They crossed the disused railway line in silence, still hoping to see the old Ford truck come rattling down the sandy trail.

"If they did set off—" Mulanda pointed to the ground in front of them "—then they didn't come this way. Those tracks are the same ones we made yesterday."

"How far is it back to that village?" Bolan asked the guide.

"See those trees," Mulanda said, nodding toward a broad belt of feverthorns well down the track. "About a mile beyond that point, I'd say. Shall I go ahead and scout around, bwana?"

"No." The American commander weighed his decision for only a second. "If they are in any kind of trouble, we might all be needed."

The two men in the back were already checking their weapons.

"Park under those trees," Bolan instructed the driver. "We'll go the rest of the way in by foot."

RAWSON COULD NOT STOP his legs from trembling. How the others could take this so calmly was beyond him. They had been forced to stand in the center of the street, in the direct sunlight, with their hands folded flat on top of their heads while Mwekango decided what to do with them.

The dark brown canvas flap of the truck's canopy had been folded up. Sitting there in the shade, one of Mwekango's men covered the five prisoners with a Soviet-made RPK. It was set on automatic. Two of the other soldiers were laughing as they waited for the forge to heat the tire iron.

Katz wondered which of the villagers had given Kambolo away. It hadn't taken long for the Leopard Patrol to round him up. They were fast and thorough—patting down each of the Phoenix men and removing their knives—but they had overlooked one small thing: none of the soldiers had asked Katz to remove the leather glove from his right hand.

He stared at the machine gunner squatting in the

truck. Katz had one shot loaded in the finger gun and he had to decide how best to use it.

The marauder manning the RPK was too far away. To be sure of a kill, Katz had to fire at almost point-blank range. He focused his attention on the officer and began to calculate their chances.

Mwekango stood with his feet apart, rocking slightly on his heels, his hand lightly slapping against his trouser leg. He missed toying with his familiar *fimbo* as he considered his options.

There was clearly an insurrection afoot. How many other mercenaries had infiltrated Kuranda? Bambabele must be mad to think his scheme would work. These men were nearly two hundred miles from the capital. But where else had they penetrated Kuranda?

There was a transmitter in the truck but Mwekango hesitated to call for the spotter plane. Yesterday General Mumungo had been at the controls himself. He had used the radio to tear a strip off the captain for his lack of success in collecting sufficient taxes. Mwekango had taken out his own frustrated rage on some nameless village back up the track. Now he had caught these foreigners. It was a coup that would restore him to Mumungo's favor.

There was little that scared Mwekango, except for his unpredictable commander in chief. The last officer in charge of the Leopard Patrol had been suspected of helping himself to some of the revenues he'd collected. Mumungo had castrated him personally.

Mwekango did not want to end up a eunuch. He

shuddered as he thought of his three mistresses. He decided to radio for the plane immediately. But there would still be time for him to do a little interrogating of his own.

He glanced across at the unit leader. The captain detected a sense of humanity lurking in the flinty depths of the older man's eyes. How long would he hold out when forced to watch his men being tortured? It would be done slowly and very carefully....

Mwekango did not want any of them dying before the plane arrived.

BOLAN AND THE NIGHT TEAM spread out in a line as they picked their way carefully through the undergrowth. The trees ahead were thinning out. Beyond the dusty vegetation, a threadbare patchwork of fields left the last half-mile to the village open.

The American pushed a thornbush aside as he considered the best way to make their final approach.

*Thwack!*

The makeshift club caught Bolan almost full across the chest.

His wounded leg buckled under him. Caught off balance, Bolan had been knocked to the ground by a burly figure hiding behind the tree. Even as he fell, Bolan thrashed out, turning the attacker's own weapon against him.

The broken branch caught the fellow in the side, smacking him hard just below the ribs. With a hiss of pain, the assailant swept the wood aside like kindling and threw himself onto the white man.

They grappled furiously, each seeking a death grip. Both were now half-blinded by the fine dust they stirred up. Bolan still had one hand on the M-16, but the rifle was jammed between their bodies. Getting a sideways hold on the weapon, he was able to use it as a lever to push his attacker off his chest.

The man sprang back and snatched up a rock. The odds were even that he'd crush Bolan's head at the same moment he would be cut down by the rifle fire. But just as he raised the heavy stone, another powerful black arm circled his throat and dragged him bodily backward.

Hearing the scramble in the bushes, Mulanda was the first to appear. He clamped his forearm across the man's windpipe and brought his knee up hard into the small of the man's back. He dropped the stone in his effort to pull Mulanda's arm away from his throat.

Mulanda was just about to finish him off. . . .

"Ziemba!"

Bolan sat up, brushing the dust from his eyes. He recognized the man now—it was the same guy the two of them had run down in the cornfield! The villager who had pleaded to come with them. It was the second time they had fought each other in as many days. Well, he had certainly recovered a more aggressive spirit.

"What the . . . ?" Encizo appeared, holding his wicked Skorpion ready to fire.

Bolan waved for him to be quiet as the Mussengamba cross-questioned Ziemba in rapid dialect.

"He says he's most sorry, bwana . . . he would not have attacked you."

"What the hell's he doing here?"

"He's been tracking the Leopard Patrol. Saw a few of them sneaking around at dawn. . . ."

More questions.

"Ziemba was making a full circle of the village." Mulanda translated the answers. "Heard us coming . . . and thought we were the rest of the Leopard men. He hid behind that tree. His only thought was to take as many with him as he could. Ziemba's quite prepared to die, bwana, but he still wants vengeance."

"It sounds as if Mumungo's men have taken the village, then," said Ohara.

"Did he hear any shots?" asked Bolan. "Was there any sound of fighting?"

Mulanda questioned the villager. Ziemba shook his head.

"Maybe the others had to withdraw to the south," suggested the Cuban. "It would explain why we haven't seen them."

Bolan shook his head. "In that case they'd have circled around through the bush and still gotten back to the road."

Ziemba spoke again and pointed to the outskirts of the village.

"There's a ravine that runs past those trees," explained Mulanda. "He was going to use it to get in close."

Bolan studied what he could through the field glasses for the moment. From this angle, the last two huts cut off his view of the blacksmith's shop and the street. But he could make out the canvas top of the.... Wait, there were two trucks! So the Leopard Patrol had seized the town. And his men were still there.

"Rafael, I want you and Keio to find that gully and sneak in as close as you can. Leave your pistols with me. I'm going to need them."

The two men nodded and unholstered their side arms.

Bolan turned to Mulanda. "Tell Ziemba to crawl across those fields and move in from the right."

The driver had hardly finished translating when Ziemba smacked his chest. He could accept the challenge. The tribesman jumped up and ran to the tree behind which he had hidden. He reappeared holding a longbow and a leather quiver full of savagely barbed arrows. The tip of each arrowhead had been dipped in the sap of the evergreen aconkanthera— one scratch of the toxin would kill a man after thirty minutes of lingering agony. Ziemba was ready for the hunt.

"Tell him he's not to fire until he hears the first shot," Bolan ordered. He turned to the others. "The same goes for you guys."

They synchronized their watches.

"I'll give you fifteen minutes to get in position," said Bolan. "Move out, there's no time to waste."

"How are we going to reach the village, bwana?" Mulanda asked, as soon as the others had left.

Bolan pointed down the track. "You and I are going to walk right in."

For once Mulanda's mouth was set in a grim line. He didn't like the sound of that idea at all.

WITH ONE HAND on the tailgate, Mwekango vaulted down onto the street. The message had been relayed. It would be at least three hours before the plane was due to arrive.

Was there anywhere it could land nearby? The captain thought the dirt road into town was sufficiently hard to serve as a temporary airstrip. In that case, he was to choose two of the prisoners to be flown back to headquarters for interrogation.

One of the troopers used a pair of tongs to pull the tire iron from the forge. The metal was glowing cherry red. It was time for the fun to start.

It was still early but already boiling hot. The mercenary invaders had been left in the sun to sweat for long enough. Mwekango nodded to his corporal to start the selection process. It would be but a cruel charade. They had discussed the matter out of earshot of the prisoners. The older man, the one who sounded a bit like an Afrikaaner, seemed the most nervous. The captain decided they were likely to break him far quicker than those other hard-eyed bastards. But Corporal Kagwa wanted to tease them some more, to play on their fears that they might be the first one to be chosen.

There was plenty of time. Mwekango did not begrudge the opportunity for his corporal to amuse himself.

The noncommissioned officer strutted down the line, pausing before each man. Kambolo stared at the ground. Kagwa stuck the wooden switch he was using as a swagger stick beneath the black prisoner's chin, and levered his head up until he could look right into the man's petrified face. It would not take long to get this one to confess what he was doing with the white dogs—in fact, it would hardly provide the squad with decent sport.

The barrel-chested foreigner who stood next to him was quite a different story. Kagwa had never before met anyone who was able to withstand their methods of questioning. If such a man existed, the corporal had the uncomfortable feeling he was looking right at him.

Rawson was standing next in line to Manning. His arm ached abominably. When the bull-necked corporal stood in front of him, he thought he was going to wet his pants. But Kagwa did not linger. He didn't want this man to know that he was the one they'd already selected.

David McCarter was worried. Not for himself—he had long ago come to terms with that. He was concerned that they would call upon Rawson as their first victim. The surveyor talked tough enough, all right, but if they put that red-hot poker near his ass he'd spill everything he knew just to save it. And that meant there'd be a full-scale sweep for Colonel Phoenix, Keio and his Cuban buddy. McCarter was not going to let that happen. He cleared his throat.

The NCO took a step closer to the captured merc. McCarter stared sheepishly at the dirt. Kagwa poked forward with his stick...and that was when McCarter pursed his lips and spit.

An ugly gobbet of phlegm landed foursquare on the corporal's toe cap.

McCarter raised his eyes to meet Kagwa's enraged expression. He gave a derisive shrug. "England expects . . . unghh!"

The noncom rammed his stick hard into the cocky pig's solar plexus. McCarter doubled forward with a gasp of pain. He stumbled, but refused to go down on his knees.

Katz dared not move. He'd shared the same worries and guessed precisely why McCarter had taken action. That crazy Englishman! Crazy as a fox. He had more guts than it was fair to expect of a man. There were eleven other troopers in Mwekango's patrol, but Katz silently swore he was going to get that corporal first.

Kagwa pulled his prized Colt from his belt and waved it in McCarter's face. He let out a torrent of invective; then, catching his breath, he turned to glance over at his commanding officer.

Mwekango nodded his approval. They could start with that impudent swine instead. It would be an object lesson for these foreigners to see how their arrogance was rewarded in the new Kuranda. And Captain Mwekango had not forgotten the question of taxes. He would line the villagers up before they started, to see what would happen to anyone who angered the Leopard Patrol. Then he'd have no trouble exacting the tribute to Buka Ntanga.

There was one thing Kagwa wanted to do first before the interrogation started. He leaned forward and hit McCarter at the base of the neck, then smashed him again with the butt of his pistol. This time the Englishman went down, collapsing groggily to his knees.

The Israeli seized the opportunity of this painful diversion to switch his hands over. The prosthetic limb, still encased in its glove, now lay on top.

Kagwa stuck out his foot, directly under McCarter's face. He was going to make the prisoner lick his boot clean.

The troopers were relaxed now, sniggering to see one of *les Affreux* groveling in front of their corporal.

Katz knew that none of them had a hope in hell. But if that was where he was going, then he'd take this swaggering noncom with him.

## 11

A movement in the back of the truck caught Katz's eye. The barrel of the machine gun was swiveling away from them. One of the men lounging in the entrance of the smithy shouted a warning.

Mwekango, inspecting the Ford and wondering where these mercenaries had stolen an old mining truck, stepped out of the shade. The interrogation was momentarily forgotten....

Another white mercenary! And this one was being prodded into the village as the prisoner of one of the villagers. The merc was a big man with a brutal expression. It looked like he'd been wounded in the leg; still, he could not have been easy to take alive.

The captain was so pleased that a villager had caught a mercenary that he hardly glanced at the native's rifle. If it had not been half-concealed by Bolan's body, he might have wondered where a poor farmer laid his hands on an AK-47.

The fifteen minutes were up; Bolan could only trust that the rest of the Phoenix team were in position. He did not have to feign his awkward gait. The cuts in his leg were burning hot, and he had three big pistols tucked uncomfortably in the back of his belt.

The men were grinning as they watched the villager

jab the prisoner with the muzzle of his rifle. Mwekango strolled toward the center of the street. He
decided they would start the questioning with this
man. Despite his limp, the big merc had the bearing
of a natural leader. A hot poker applied to that leg
might produce some interesting answers.

With an evil sneer, Corporal Kagwa half turned to
gloat at Katz. What the...! He had dared to unfold
his hands! And why was the man pointing at him so
accusingly?

Kagwa found out as the tip of that gloved finger
exploded.

The corporal's right eye mushed into a spurting red
crater.

Bolan had stepped to one side. Both hands flew behind his back and reappeared holding two Colt auto-
matics.

"Gary!" He threw one to Manning as he took a
left-handed bead on the nearest guard.

His sideways movement had left Mulanda with a
clear field of fire. The first burst from the Kalash-
nikov caught Mwekango in the shoulder. The captain
spun around from the impact and crashed into the
dust. The tracker continued to blast at the truck,
blowing the machine gunner back into the shadowy
recess. He kept on firing.

Less than five seconds had elapsed since Katz blew
the back off Kagwa's head. The members of the
much vaunted Leopard Patrol were not used to the
idea of anyone ever fighting back. They were utterly
rattled that these men had taken the initiative against
them.

Seeing both their leader and his second-in-command cut down, the rest of the squad were left in total chaos. Three of the troopers who had been standing behind the prisoners took to their heels and ran for the cover of the nearest alleyway between the huts.

Katz's personalized firepower was limited to a single shot. There was neither time nor point in trying to reload. A fourth man was trying to line up Bolan in his sights. Katz simply spun around and grabbed the rifleman in a terminal bear hug. The man dropped his weapon as he was crushed within that iron grip.

McCarter had snatched up Kagwa's Colt and shot one of the guards as he dived for cover behind the old Ford. The damn piece jammed! He drew the slide to the rear and knocked out the stuck case. By the time it was recocked, the other soldier had fled behind the blacksmith's shop.

Within a split second of catching the pistol Bolan had thrown to him, Manning snapped off a round at the guy by the forge. The trooper was knocked back across the white-hot charcoal and started screaming horribly. The Canadian did not put him out of his scorching misery. Manning whirled around, dropped to one knee and took aim at the last of the soldiers vanishing between the thatched huts.

Katz was still holding the struggling trooper in both arms. McCarter plucked the man's own bayonet from its scabbard and punched it in hard between his ribs. Only then did Katz let go.

The three men who had scurried behind the houses just kept on running. They headed for the stand of acacia trees. It looked like refuge from the bloodbath that had been unleashed. It wasn't—Encizo and Ohara were waiting for them.

Bolan smiled grimly as he heard the crack of Keio's rifle followed by the ugly chatter of the Skorpion.

Mwekango was not dead. He crawled toward the shelter of the smithy. Only Mulanda saw him, and he was reloading. The wounded Leopard Patrol leader made it behind the safety of the thick mud walls.

He slithered over the rear wall of the blacksmith's shop. There were only open fields beyond, but at least there was no one in sight. Clutching his bleeding shoulder, he began to stumble forward.

Then, seeming to rise out of the ground itself like the dusty apparition of an avenging ghost, Ziemba appeared. Mwekango stood on uncertain, shaky legs, trying to find the strength to raise his shattered arm. The black warrior used only one arrow. It caught the leader of the Leopard Patrol dead in the throat.

Mwekango's eyes were crossed, trying to look at the thin quivering shaft that protruded below his chin. He couldn't scream—the barbed point had shredded his vocal cords. Ziemba watched as the captain toppled forward in the dirt.

It was done. Justice had been served.

"THERE ARE THREE MORE back there," called out Ohara, as he emerged into the street.

Katz completed the body count. "We're one short."

Mulanda found the tracks.

"He should have been mine," confessed McCarter, rubbing his shoulder, "but my gun stovepiped."

The Leopard trooper must have hidden while Ziemba settled his score with the captain. Then he took off for the distant scrub. All he left behind were deep toe indentations.

"He was running for his life," said Mulanda.

"I expect he'll throw away his uniform and melt into the bush." Nonetheless Bolan checked the terrain through his glasses. "I doubt if he'll want to confess to Mumungo that he was the only one who survived."

Bolan found the first-aid kit in the back of the Ford. He redressed his leg wound properly this time as he listened to Katz complete a quiet report of what had taken place. There would be no postmortem; no apportioning of blame for this morning's bloody showdown.

It was another round in the everlasting war.

And they had come out ahead.

That was all that counted.

But their principal objective remained unchanged. It was time for them to head north, to cross that desert again, and press hard on the heels of Yagoda and Scarr.

"Thanks," McCarter said, touching Katz gently on the sleeve as their two black drivers passed carrying the body of Corporal Kagwa. "I wish I'd had the pleasure."

"You can do the same for me sometime," shrugged Katz.

"Hey, *pescado!*" The ex-SAS officer turned away to greet Rafael Encizo. "Did you have a good night's hunting?"

The Cuban nodded. He looked at the row of bodies stretched out by the smithy. The cream of Mumungo's personal guard lay curdled in their own blood. Enzizo shook his head and said gruffly, "I knew we shouldn't have left you...."

"Well, we had to stage something just to get hold of that lovely truck!"

Enzizo grunted. He never knew when to believe the Englishman. It was Bolan who smiled. McCarter was right. They had at least solved the transport problem.

"Get everything loaded into their truck," he ordered. He glanced up at the huge clouds sailing in from the southwest. The villagers would have to take care of the bodies. "Come on, Kambolo, hop to it. You, too, Rawson! Pull your weight. It's going to pour in a moment."

They were bumping over the railway tracks, with the Land Rover a couple of hundred yards ahead, when the first big droplets streaked down across the windshield.

THE PILOT'S HANDS were clenched around the controls of the Pilatus PC-6. He flinched as Mumungo cursed bitterly once more.

The rainstorm had passed. It had spent its squalling fury against the slopes of the Mambosso hills, leaving the ground sodden, steaming and far too soft to take the weight of the spotter plane.

"Circle the village again!" ordered the general.

"Yes, sir, but I don't think there's anywhere dry enough for us to land."

Mumungo shifted his considerable bulk and stared

out of the side window. The thatched roofs were clustered directly below them. There was nothing else to be seen. Just a broken-down old truck parked at one end of the street. There was certainly no sign of Captain Mwekango and his men.

And there had been no further reports over the radio. That puzzled Mumungo. The pilot called in to headquarters and double-checked; but they hadn't heard anything on the alternate frequencies either.

"Fly up toward that pass," hissed Mumungo, spittle flecking the corners of his fleshy lips. He could barely constrain his rage.

The pilot banked away to the north.

MULANDA'S VOLLEY had killed the machine gunner, knocked out one of the taillights and smashed the radio equipment. Apart from that, the Leopard Patrol's vehicle was undamaged. It ran like a dream compared to the old Ford that Rawson had supplied. And they made excellent time on their run across the Forge. Even though they had to follow the main track, Phoenix Force reached the Shoba Well in just under three hours.

Bolan had redistributed the team. Mulanda was driving the Land Rover, but now he carried Kambolo, Ziemba and Encizo as passengers. In acquiring Captain Mwekango's leopard spot trousers and cap for himself—the bush jacket was far too messed up to be salvaged—the Mussengamba driver unwittingly contributed to the effect that Bolan hoped would confuse any further witness to their progress into northeast Kuranda.

Rawson was at the wheel of the truck. Bolan and Keio shared the cab with him. Hence the two potential troublemakers were split up and under watchful eyes. And Bolan was going to keep it that way until the end of the mission.

He called a halt at the water hole to see if any evidence of their night raid had been left behind.

"Police the area," ordered Bolan. "Rawson, bury those ration containers and that cigarette pack."

Manning shoveled sand over the dead ashes of the Angolans' campfire.

Whatever the final outcome, Bolan did not want what had happened here ever to be reconstructed.

This was a private war.

Mulanda finished refilling the tanks and put down the gas can. He pointed to the top of Pyramid Hill and began to mime Bolan's struggle with the leopard.

Far from being humbled by what had befallen him that morning, Kambolo's relief at being rescued seemed only to have made him cockier. It was the second time he'd had to listen to Mulanda's enthusiastic account of the fight. And he still did not look as if he believed it.

The tracker tugged at his sleeve, inviting him to climb up the steep slope and see for himself. It was less than half a mile. But Kambolo shrugged him off with a contemptuous sneer. It was the superior disdain that only a "civilized" native held for the "ignorant" tribesmen like Mulanda.

Katz caught Bolan's eye and shook his head. The two men had the same thoughts. Intolerance seemed to fester here. The Israeli stalked off in disgust.

"Come, let me show you," insisted the tracker. "You'll see!"

He turned to the commander, pleading for just a few minutes to escort Kambolo to the scene of the duel. Bolan denied him. "Have you checked the rads, the tires...? Kambolo, make sure all the canteens are filled."

Mulanda looked disgruntled but did as he was told. One did not argue with the *bwana mukubwa*. The other man went to fetch the water.

Bolan himself had not given another thought to the conflict he'd so narrowly won against the marauding predator. He did not dwell on what might have happened. His fighting instincts were fully focused on the moment, where they were needed.

He did not question the strength that had been given him to overpower the beast, the skills that had saved him in a hundred firefights, or the tenacity to keep battling against the crushing odds of chaos. They came from the deepest wellsprings of his being. And beyond....

Long ago he had chosen.

And he was chosen.

Fate had dictated he be reborn as John Phoenix. He was called upon to be the cutting edge in these few rounds of the historic struggle against evil and injustice. Bolan had vowed to carry the fight until his dying breath. That was his commitment, his purpose. But he also knew when the final moment came, it would be the very force that propelled him that would also discharge him from this noble service.

Death held no private, unspoken terrors for The

Executioner...and that was why he was free to live large, to live in this present moment.

Most people chose to live small—some even settled for that quiet desperation of a death in life—but it was not his way.

He was not immortal.

Death would claim him. He knew that.

But when Bolan met his Maker, he'd look Him straight in the eye. Until then, he chose life. It was the only way he knew.

"Mack!" It was Yakov's voice. "Over here."

Bolan pushed through the tangled bushes to the spot where the older man was poking about with his cane at the edge of a shallow fissure. "Look at this."

The bodies had been laid out end to end, loosely covered with rocks, brush and a few spadefuls of sand. The jackals had already found them—perhaps they had been scared from their feast by the arrival of Phoenix Force.

"Scarr must have left in an awful hurry," said the Israeli.

"Looks that way," agreed Bolan. "Time we got going too. We'll leave these to the scavengers."

They continued on as before.

McCarter stared out of the back of the truck at the blasted landscape of Devil's Forge: weirdly eroded rocks bent and broken under the crushing weight of the sun.

"Reminds me of Aden," the Englishman said. "Up near the Yemen border. Bad country. How much farther does this go on for, Katz?"

"We've got about another hour of it, according to Mulanda."

Well, I'll be glad when...hey, what's that? Look, back there!"

"Looks like we've got company," said Katz. He went forward and tapped on the interconnecting window. "Don't look over your shoulder, Mack, but there's a light plane gaining on us fast."

"Okay, keep your eye on it. Rawson, sound your horn to warn the others."

"I think it's one of those Swiss jobs—a Porter," called out McCarter, pulling down the canvas flap.

"A Pilatus Porter," relayed Katz.

The plane flew over them as low as the pilot dared, then climbed and banked in an uncertain circle.

"That's the Leopard Patrol's spotter plane," said Rawson.

"Take it easy," Bolan told him. "They don't have a clue what's happened down here. Just keep driving."

The Mussengamba tracker in the lead vehicle took off his new cap and waved as the Porter made a second pass.

Bolan was forced to smile. "Now Mulanda's got them more confused than ever."

This time the plane flew on steadily northward.

"Damn," swore Rawson. "They're going to check out where it is we're heading in such a hurry."

**12**

The loose folds of Scarr's shirt stuck clammily to his chest, as much from nervousness as from the increasing humidity. But he was glad to be quit of the desert. That arid landscape of burnt ochers, gray browns and dirty rust gave way first to grasses and green scrub, then to vine-hung trees and tangled undergrowth spilling out onto the road.

The driver downshifted as the gradient became steeper.

"It gets easier up ahead, where it runs alongside the railroad," commented Scarr. The details of that earlier drive were etched in his memory.

Yagoda, positioned in the middle of the bench seat, studied the map. Already he was looking for an alternate route back from this Blood River country.

The South African turned to glance out the side window. He stared long in the mirror and wondered once again who it could be that dogged their tracks.

Pandemonium had threatened in the predawn darkness when an Angolan sentry had stumbled first on one body, then a second and a third.... Sergeant Sanchez was the worst corpse of all. And the NCO was lying only inches from Yagoda.

The Russian, although shaken, had not lost his

cool—Scarr conceded that. He'd kept the Cubans in line, and they had leaned on the blacks. By the first glimmer of daybreak their losses had been assessed, the damaged tires replaced and the bodies buried. The men who had been on duty knew they would have to face punishment.

Yagoda called Scarr back to the trucks as camp was set up. He had been scouting around the base of the hill. They had to make up for lost time, Yagoda explained edgily, and ordered the Stars to roll. They moved out quickly.

Scarr said nothing of what he had found in the damp sand at the far end of the water hole. Yagoda and the Cubans believed they were the victims of renegade tribesmen. The Angolans confirmed it. That was what their silent attackers had wanted them to think. But Brendan Scarr knew that Bushmen did not wear jungle boots with thick rubber cleats!

He only caught glimpses of the two trucks behind in the shuddering image of the side mirror. But someone else was back there, too. Who could it be? And how close were they? For now, Scarr remained silent. Whoever it was might prove to be his ace in the hole.

They were less than two hours' drive from the spot where he had left the loot. Scarr had to think fast on how he would make good his escape. He was quite certain that Yagoda had no intention of taking him back to Angola—at least, not alive. Even if he did, there was no guarantee that Scarr would then be set free.

The mercenary reflected on his checkered past. He could draw some confidence from it.

The blacks had never been able to kill him. Vandergriff's men could not catch him. Even Quita prison hadn't killed him. Brendan Scarr had outwitted them all.

Lying and double-dealing, running, fighting when cornered, Scarr had stayed alive this long. It would take a lot tougher bastard than Colonel Boris Yagoda to finish him off.

"Hey, look at that!" Scarr pointed ahead of them. A tiny duiker had scampered across the trail and plunged into the brush. Yagoda missed it. The Afrikaaner sneered. Yagoda didn't have the feel for this sort of country.

"Watch where you're going!" snapped the Russian, when the driver drifted too close to the edge of the track.

Yagoda felt as if he were walking on a tightrope. It was not the first time in his career that he'd had this uneasy feeling, treading a dangerous line between the natural caution of the diplomatic experts and the more ambitious demands of the Second Directorate on Tekstilshchikov Street. But none of those bureaucrats were out here in the field. They were never around when the dirty work had to be done.

But Boris Yagoda had built his reputation as a man willing to take chances. He had experienced this same momentary queasiness when he staged the car "accident" that settled the Sol Yurkevitch affair. His immediate supervisor, Krasnov, had dissociated himself from Yagoda. But when the Western press swallowed the story of the dissident's unfortunate death, Yagoda did not have to share the accolades with his boss. He had been promoted to colonel.

After an immersion course in Spanish, which added to his working knowledge of English and French, Yagoda shipped out for Angola. He thought it would be a better opportunity to display his talents than the thankless war in Afghanistan. But at this moment he was beginning to wonder if he had made the right choice this time.

Four men lost and they had not yet reached the mercenary's hoard. Yagoda lit a cigarette. He would issue a suitably flattering statement on behalf of the Angolan soldiers, praising their sacrifice for the cause of revolution. As for the Cubans... what did it matter? They were expendable. That was precisely why the Russians were using them here. He took a drag deep into his lungs. He felt better already. And it would improve his mood even more to be rid of this condescending South African.

"I told you, it's leveling out." Scarr pointed through the trees to their right. "See, there's the railway tracks."

The trail ran parallel to the railroad lines for about four miles, until they reached a large clearing. Evidently it had once been a loading yard.

"There's several mines around here," explained Scarr. "The major mining companies shared this facility for shipping out their ore."

Sheds of corrugated iron were rusted and overgrown with heaps of vines and matted vegetation. Yagoda called a halt and immediately wished he hadn't—this place smelled of decay and disuse. He had the uncomfortable feeling they were being watched.

The men climbed out to stretch their legs.

Scarr was relieving himself at the side of the track, when his head cocked to óne side. Suddenly he shouted, "Get those trucks under cover! Quick, into the trees!"

Yagoda whirled around. How dared he give orders! But then he had heard it, too. A light plane was approaching. It was droning low over the treetops. Yagoda signaled frantically to confirm Scarr's instructions.

The Cuban drivers jumped back into their cabs. One of the Stars protested at being started up so soon after being shut off—it stalled.

"Push it!" screamed Yagoda, throwing the two nearest Angolans against the rear end. Three more joined them. They rolled the truck under the protective canopy of foliage just as the plane roared over the clearing at three hundred feet.

Everyone froze. They stood in absolute silence, watching as the plane turned and made another pass over the railway yard.

Had the pilot seen them?

It circled again.

"Who is it?" asked Yagoda.

Scarr shrugged, scarcely able to suppress a grin. He was pleased to see the KGB officer looking so rattled—he might get careless. The aircraft passed directly above them. They waited, still not moving. This time it did not come back.

"Everyone into the trucks," ordered Yagoda. He turned to Scarr. "Get us out of here!"

The guide pointed to a dark opening between the trees on the far side of the clearing. "Follow that side road. It'll take us across the river. Don't worry, Colonel, we're almost there."

"This is where I'm officially supposed to be," snorted Rawson, letting go of the wheel to indicate the twin steel tracks now running parallel to the narrow road. "I filed a report saying I would be checking out the condition of the Makala rail system when I came to meet you guys. It seemed like a good cover story at the time."

The note of cynical regret in his voice left no doubt that Luke Rawson wished he had never got involved with Phoenix Force.

There was no way that Yagoda and his men could have left the trail. If they had pulled off into the bush, then their exit would have been marked through the thick profusion of plant life that crowded the path on either side.

Bolan stared at the twin ribbons of railroad line through the flickering shadows of the encroaching jungle. "Where do they lead to?"

"This one curves south right around the back of the Mambosso range—we crossed over it outside that Baluba village—then it goes on down through the towns along the Kasai," explained the surveyor. "The other track runs east. It was used to pick up mahogany from the lumber camps along the border."

"Is it still used?"

"Not often. Not much of anything is operating in this bloody country since Buka Ntanga was made king." Rawson kept a careful eye that he did not tread too close on the heels of the Land Rover. There was obviously something on his mind. "Well, I can't go back now. They'll find the company truck sooner or later, then there'll be a search for Mumungo's men...."

"I guess you'll have to come out with us," Bolan reassured him. "I'm sure the prime minister will see you are well rewarded for helping us. Anyway, once Bambabele is restored to power you'll be able to.... Damn, it's coming back again!"

The plane was flying south directly above the track. They were caught in the open with no time to hide. Bolan got a glimpse of an angry black face staring down from the copilot's window as the aircraft wobbled low overhead. Then it was gone. The pilot made a correctional trim and kept on flying south, away from them.

The men in the lead vehicle looked back but the Phoenix leader leaned from the cab and waved them on. "Keep going!"

"Funny he didn't come back to check us out again," observed Rawson, gnawing at his lower lip.

"Either he's seen what he wanted to ahead of us," said Bolan, unfolding the map, "or he's damn near out of fuel. Maybe both. Where's the nearest spot he could gas up that plane?"

"There's a small airstrip to the southeast, near Mabuti, but that's just to serve the lumber camps...." Bolan traced along the thin line of the railroad track until he found the spot. Rawson jerked his thumb over his left shoulder. "I'd say he'll head for the base at Usomo. It's to the west. There's an army camp there."

"So he could bring back a few truckloads of reinforcements!" said Ohara. "Direct them in from the air."

Rawson swallowed nervously. When he first heard about this mission, he saw it only as a way to feather his nest for early retirement. Bloody hell, he hadn't figured on ending up in a full-scale shooting war.

"It would take four or five hours for the first troops to reach this far," said Bolan, studying the twisting roads that reached up into the Makala high country. "We've still got time to do what we came for."

"Yeah, but they're right between us and the plane on Lake Baruka," snapped Rawson. "How are we going to get away then, eh? Besides, they could have alerted the Usomo camp by radio. Those soldiers could already be on their way up here."

Bolan made no response. The same thing had occurred to him. He studied the map, figuring out a contingency plan. "What's this just ahead of us? Looks like a marshaling yard."

"That's just what it is, or used to be," explained the surly surveyor. "INGOT and Kuranda Lumber shared it to ship their product down to the city. See where the trees are thinning out...."

The rusted hulk of a North British 4-8-0 locomotive sat in the corner of the broad clearing. The old engine was slowly surrendering to the creepers that were reclaiming the yard. The roof of one of the large tin sheds already sagged under the sheer weight of the vines that had overgrown it. Only one of the sheds had held its own against the relentless vegetation.

Mulanda had stopped the Land Rover in the center of the track and jumped out.

"What have you found?" Bolan called out as he climbed down from the cab.

The Mussengamba guide pointed to the broken ferns beside the road. The flowers had been crushed and the leaf mold under the trees retained the imprints of tires and combat boots. They were still on the right track. Scarr must have pulled the unit off the road here.

"Do you think the plane saw them, too?" Katz wondered aloud.

"We'll have to assume so," said Bolan. "Mulanda, scout around and find out where they've gone."

Ziemba joined Mulanda in scouting out the roads that led away from the far end of the yard.

Rawson was looking at the tracks. One pair of rails was shinier than the others. They led directly into the nearby shed.

"Bloody uncomfortable in the back," McCarter complained in a loud voice. "Think I'll take a leak."

Bolan caught his signal. As McCarter vanished into the greenery, he made a small encircling gesture with his fingers then pointed toward the engine shed.

"Okay, men, I'm going for a stroll," Bolan murmured. "Act normal, but keep your hands near your weapons."

He walked across the rails, faking a casual interest in the marshaling yard. His ears were alert for the slightest sound of whatever had alarmed his English colleague. Deciding he had walked far enough, Bolan turned and quickly approached the shed from the blind side. There was a door inset a few feet from the corner.

Manning and Encizo appeared to be inspecting the Land Rover. Katz lit a cigarette as he listened to Keio; both men seemed relaxed. But they were all ready for instant action as David McCarter emerged from the bushes and crept along the side of the shed, his back flattened to the wall.

He reached a dust-encrusted window, smashed it with his rifle and poked the muzzle through. "Right, you, outside! Easy now. . . I've got you covered every step of the way."

The door creaked open. A man stepped out, blinking in the sunlight. He was about sixty, bald except for a fringe of white curls at the back, and dressed in a much-darned pair of blue coveralls.

"You can put your hands down, old-timer," said Bolan. "What are you doing here?"

"I live here," the man replied with quiet dignity. "I look after *tembo*."

Bolan didn't understand.

"*Tembo* means elephant," Rawson explained to Bolan.

The old railwayman glanced around at the soldiers who now surrounded him in a loose semicircle. He almost did a double-take when he saw the INGOT surveyor. "Rawson bwana, is that you, Mr. Rawson?"

"Oduka, you old rascal! What are you up to?"

"Same as always," replied Oduka, as he unlatched one of the shed doors and dragged it open. "Keeping *tembo* clean. Taking her for a run now and then. Waiting for the mines to be reopened."

By bush locomotive standards, she was indeed an elephant! Oduka's *tembo*, a 1933 Beyer Peacock 4-6-4, stood gleaming softly in the musty shadows.

"Still looks as good as the last time I saw her!" exclaimed Rawson. The railway worker's dedication seemed to have rekindled some of his own professional enthusiasm.

"That must have been five years ago," said Oduka.

"Is there anyone else around?" asked Bolan.

Oduka shook his head. "I live here alone. Sometimes I take *tembo* down to Mabuti for supplies, but no one comes up here anymore...that is, until...."

"You saw the other soldiers?"

Oduka nodded.

"They took the left-hand fork through those trees," announced Mulanda, returning from his scouting expedition.

"Three trucks full of men. I saw them. They drove on toward the river," confirmed Oduka. "But it's a dead end. The road runs out about six miles past the bridge."

"At the old Copperhill workings?" asked Rawson.

"Yes, bwana. But they were shut down even before Mumungo seized power." Oduka spit at mentioning the general's name. "Copperhill closed the mines even before my time. There's nothing up there!''

''Thanks, Mr. Oduka,'' said Bolan. He signaled for the others to get back aboard the vehicles. ''We better take a look at what they've found.''

Oduka decided it was time to stoke up *tembo*'s fire. He needed supplies; he would make a trip down to Mabuti. Much as the railwayman hated the usurper Mumungo, this was not his fight.

THE DOWNPOUR HAD STOPPED, but the driver left the wipers running—the water would drip down on them from the trees for quite a while yet. Yagoda ground out his cigarette. He did not like the jungle.

The rainy season extended all year; at least some fell every day on these slopes. This regular precipitation nurtured a luxuriant display of plant life. Lillies and violets bloomed in the rich humus, rotting logs were covered with a vivid carpet of moss, and thick lianas hung from the sapele...layer upon layer of verdant vegetation stretching up to the dense canopy nearly a hundred twenty feet above the trail.

The Russian checked the time. Their progress was too slow. It was nearly an hour since they left that bridge behind and they could not have covered more than five miles. What if that plane came back?

''Stop, Hector,'' Scarr ordered the driver. ''I...I think this is it.'' His voice was shaky. He had waited a long time for this moment.

The South African pointed out of the open window. Yagoda followed the line he was indicating. He could only make out a reddish orange bulk under a tangle of creepers.

"Welcome to Copperhill, Colonel. Looks like the jungle is reclaiming all the equipment."

The undergrowth was thinner here, of more recent growth than back down the trail. Rusting metal hoppers, winches and scoops were vanishing beneath the choking press of the foliage.

Scarr pointed to a dark opening half concealed by a screen of bushes. "The stuff's over there...or it should be. I parked the truck in the entrance to that old mine."

**13**

The steep-sided gorge of the upper Makala was a wild and beautiful place. It was a deep dogleg of a chasm. A bridge, suspended high above the raging torrent, spanned the river at the bend. Cliffs, on both sides of the river, rose almost sheer out of the water for two hundred feet or more, but only odd patches of bare rock showed through; for the most part it was over-grown with tangled clumps of moist vegetation.

Mack Bolan and the men of Phoenix Force, the three blacks and Luke Rawson stood at the end of the bridge and looked down.

The air was filled with the shrilling sounds of myriad insects. Living clouds of butterflies swarmed over the colorful foliage. And flocks of birds exe-cuted precision maneuvers as they swooped and rose on the thermals generated within the humid canyon.

"Easy to see why they call it the River of Blood," remarked McCarter. The spuming torrent below was stained dark with the rich mineralized sludge washed down in the runoff, as if the Makala still flowed rust-red with the blood of those nameless men who had died working the diamond digs, lumber camps and copper mines.

Billows of oily smoothness broke into white froth

as they dashed onto the rocks scattered among the shallows. Encizo watched the twisting, racing rapids for a moment. He shook his head at the river's mindless fury. "There's no way a plane could ever land down there."

"Or anywhere else remotely nearby," added Bolan, pointing to the dense pack of forest giants that crowned the banks on either side.

The bridge itself was a rickety suspension construction—strong enough in its time perhaps, but that was long past. The uneven wooden walkway was supported by corroded metal cables. Some of the crosspieces had rotted or broken, and had then been replaced with trees felled in the surrounding woods and roughly split apart as planking. In one or two places even creosote-coated railroad ties had been used to repair the bridge. Bolan watched where he placed his foot every step of the way across. Only Gary Manning accompanied him.

It did not take the two men long to complete a preliminary reconnaissance. Bolan soon reappeared at the far end of the bridge and shouted across, "Okay, Yakov, this is it! Get that stuff unloaded and start setting up."

It was only sixty yards across the swaying span but the American had to raise his voice above the noise level of the bustling, vibrant gorge. However, the staggered ranks of huge fluted tree trunks formed an effective shield to prevent his shouted instructions from carrying beyond the immediate area of the bridge.

He turned away again and walked up the road,

counting his paces as he measured off a selected distance. Manning scrambled along through the undergrowth trying to keep up.

"That's about it," Bolan said, turning to face the blank green wall of scrub that edged the track. "Anything suitable up there?"

Manning judged he was in line with the spot chosen by the colonel. "Yes. I think this mahogany looks big enough."

Bolan did not try to break through to join Manning, as the other man notched a mark into the trunk. On no account did he want the underbrush disturbed—there should be nothing that would give them away.

He strolled back to the bridge checking both sides for potential spots to station the men, then waited for Manning to retrace his steps.

"There's a small depression here—be a good pit for the automatic weapons," Manning called out. "It has a clear field of . . . . Geez!"

The Canadian bounded out onto the track. "A bloody, great mottled snake. . . hardly saw the damn thing!"

"Gabon viper, I expect," Bolan remarked dryly, trying not to smile at seeing the burly engineer as shaken as if he'd seen a ghost. "This is just their kind of country."

"Lethal?"

"Fatal," Bolan said, nodding. "Almost always."

By the time they had walked back across the bridge, Manning had recovered his usual taciturn poise. He went straight to the cases of explosives and began sorting out what he needed.

Encizo had already made a careful inspection of the posts supporting the cables. "I'll have to swing down underneath and mine the concrete reinforcements."

Ohara went to fetch a coil of rope from the back of the Land Rover. The Phoenix men were working together smoothly as a team; it was the others who needed to be told what to do.

"Kambolo, give Gary a hand with that C-4," ordered Bolan. The black driver looked startled. He opened his mouth to protest. The American would have none of it. "Yes, you. Take that stuff over to the other side!"

Hearing the stern instructions, Rawson skipped nimbly toward the Rover. "I'll get the transport turned around."

"Mulanda, give him a hand. Hide the truck in those bushes there. Make sure everything's set to roll when we need it."

Ziemba had not needed to be shouted at, he was pitching in already. The big villager was carrying spare ammunition and a case of grenades across the swaying bridge. Kambolo and the Canadian were ahead of him.

Bolan was going to risk as few men as he dared on the far side of the river. He had the M-16 sloped on his shoulder as he strode back to the bridgehead, where Encizo was checking to see that the line was secure before lowering himself over the side.

Katz stood in Bolan's path, the thumb of his good hand hooked in his clutch belt. With the slightest shake of his head, he said quietly. "You're not leaving me out of it, Mack."

"Wouldn't dream of it," replied Bolan, instantly making the decision. He turned to McCarter, who was setting up the captured RPK. "You're in charge.

"After you." Bolan gestured toward the planks. The Israeli led the way over. It was hardly wide enough for a truck, and even then it would have to be guided at a walking pace. And no one in their right mind would allow more than one vehicle to cross at a time.

Bolan steadied himself against one of the side cables and peered over to watch the Cuban dangling in front of the rock face, packing his deadly putty into cracks around the concrete buttresses.

"The bird's coming back!" yelled McCarter, pointing to the western leg of the canyon. Bolan was still covered by the nearby outcrop that marked the bend in the Makala gorge. He ran to the far side of the bridge.

Encizo froze, spread-eagled against the rock. The plane was skimming along slightly above the treetops. It would clear the bridge with only a few feet to spare.

Bolan reached the dense shrubbery on the north rim, remembered the snake Manning had seen and plunged into the bushes on the right.

Hanging on the end of his safety line, Rafael Encizo felt totally exposed and vulnerable. Surely the pilot or his spotter must be staring straight at him! But the explosives expert's camouflage blended per-

fectly with the gray rock, green moss, orange lichen
and the banded shadows of the bridge.

In any case the flier's attention was devoted to
navigating the turn in the Makala Gorge safely. The
single-engined Porter filled the canyon with a roaring
reverberation of echoes. At this close range they
could have concentrated enough firepower to bring it
down, but they were after a bigger prize. So Bolan
watched as the plane flashed past, climbed away
from the river and headed north.

Encizo steadied himself against the turbulent back-
wash. He took a deep breath, pulled another one-
pound block of plastic explosive from his satchel and
packed it into the cracks around the pillar support.

"You DIDN'T BURY IT?" Yagoda sounded incredu-
lous, as if it offended his sense of efficiency.

Scarr offered no explanation. With the Simbas hot
on his heels, there had not been time...nor anyone
left alive to help him. "It's still here, isn't it?"

The tires were gone, gnawed away by countless
curious, hungry teeth over the years. The axles had
settled deep in the leaf mold that had drifted into the
entrance of the long-abandoned mine. The truck sat
slightly tilted to one side, but otherwise intact.

The renegade tugged at the canvas cover and the
rotted fabric fell away in his hands. Yagoda peered
over his shoulder to see that the safe-deposit boxes,
once neatly stacked, were scattered on the truckbed.
Twenty-eight locked metal containers, their black
enamel finish dulled by the passage of years, were lying right where Scarr had left them—just as he had

promised the Russian. He breathed a sigh of relief and walked back out into the open clearing.

"Bring that truck over here. Back it up to the entrance," instructed Yagoda. He knew the men had been speculating on what they would find, but he certainly wasn't going to risk opening the boxes here. He swallowed hard, stifling his own impulse to check them out immediately.

Scarr looked up at the sky as he first hunched then relaxed his shoulders, feeling the flush of vindication after the tensions of the past few days. He had not been allowed a weapon for the duration of the journey. But now Private Pablo Lomez had gotten careless! The Cuban soldier walked over to the mine for a closer look at the treasure truck and left his rifle leaning against a fallen log.

As nonchalantly as he could, Scarr began to edge nearer to the forgotten gun. It was the chance he was looking for...seize it and run! Yagoda would not risk chasing him far through this impenetrable forest.

He circled slowly toward the log Lomez had been using as a backrest. It went against the grain to abandon the diamonds, but saving his own skin came first.

The forest canopy had muffled the sound of Mumungo's plane. One of the Angolans fell as he swung around pointing up, shouting a warning that came too late. His bellow of surprise was drowned out by the 340-horsepower engine.

The surrounding greenery was still riffled by the propwash as the spotter plane turned for a second, closer inspection of the mine workings.

"Get the last of those boxes transferred," Yagoda yelled. "Scarr! Come over here!"

Lomez knocked into the merc as he scrambled past to retrieve his rifle. Scarr had made his move too late. He had no choice but to obey Yagoda.

As half a dozen of the Angolans formed a human chain to shift the last of the cargo into the back of Yagoda's truck, the KGB officer unfolded his map. "If we get back across the river and go due east, how far is it to the border?"

"About three hours if we hit the Mabuti road."

Scarr had to raise his voice above the sound of the plane. Yagoda glanced upward for a moment. He was glad that he'd brought two additional truckloads of troops. It looked as if they might be needed now. Even under cover of darkness, they might have to fight their way out.

"Can we then swing south along the edge of Shaba province and get back into Angola that way?"

Scarr wasn't sure, but he was not going to admit it. Yagoda needed the mercenary alive. "Yes," he said, nodding decisively. "I know a route through there."

He reached up to swing the cab door open.

"No—" Yagoda laid a hand on his arm "—this time you ride in the truck behind until we reach that railway depot . . . then you can take the lead."

"GARY HAS GOT THE TREE all wired to blow," reported Katz. "He wants to know if you'd like him to place a charge in the middle of the road."

"No time for that," said Bolan. The unpredictable breezes swirling around the canyon area had shifted yet again and they both caught the faraway drone of the Swiss-made spotter plane. "Just make sure everyone's in position, Yakov."

Time was running against them now. Mumungo's troops were bound to be on the way, but just how far had they got?

This covert operation had been launched with the express purpose of preventing the Russians from exploiting the local tensions to their advantage. Bolan remembered Brognola's lecture on how at any moment the U.S. could be drawn into a new peace-keeping role in the ongoing Namibian crisis, and Moscow would love to aggravate that situation by opening old sores. Now their position looked as if it might provoke an ugly international confrontation. And they could expect no help from Washington. Phoenix Force operated alone in the field—that was their mandate.

Bolan looked south across the suspension bridge. He knew where his men were positioned, but he could see no sign of them.

McCarter was on the left with the Soviet machine gun. On the Englishman's immediate flank, Ohara was ready to back him up with grenades. And Encizo was standing by at the detonator control. He had not had to tell them to keep a close watch on Rawson.

It was time for Bolan to make sure his own team was as well concealed.

At the end of the bridge where he stood was a flattened pan of hard dirt about thirty feet across by fifty. It quickly narrowed as the road led away from the edge of the gorge, angling up through the trees to the right. After a quarter of a mile it twisted again, crossed over a ridge and ran north toward the Copperhill mines. Kambolo was keeping watch at the bend.

The underbrush was not so dense back in the perpetual green twilight under the trees. But where the light penetrated, around the bridgehead area and along the trail itself, the vegetation was thick and luxuriant, affording the ambush team perfect cover.

Bolan walked slowly up the path to make certain they had left no sign that might warn a watchful enemy of their presence; then, just as carefully, he began to retrace his steps.

"All set here!" Manning's muffled voice came from the bushes.

Only when Ziemba actually shook his bow in a defiant salute could the American spot the ebony warrior perched among the branches of a shorter tree festooned with vines.

Katz stood waiting beside the path. He gestured to the rotten hulk of a fallen log. "I'll take the other side over there," he said.

"Okay, I'll cover the bridge approach itself."

"They're coming!" It was Kambolo. He was racing down the path. He stumbled over a root but, with arms windmilling, managing not to fall. "I saw the first truck coming over the hill," he panted.

Kambolo was sweating profusely, more from fear than sudden exertion. Why had Rawson brought along a citified black who was less at home in the bush than any of the whites on the team? For one split second Bolan recalled an image of Malakesi in his tailored business suit and wondered how Bambabele's aide had fared in the guerrilla days of their original campaign. "Come on, you better hide with me."

The sharp metallic click of Katz's signaler carried clearly across the gorge. The Israeli thought he heard McCarter cock the RPK, then he turned to take up his station.

Kambolo nervously tugged a handkerchief from his trouser pocket and dabbed at his shiny brow as he followed the big foreigner behind the cover of the bushes.

Neither of them noticed he had dropped his cigarette lighter in the middle of the track.

THAT THERE WAS simply nowhere to land the Porter did not frustrate Mumungo as much as the fact that he could not even begin to comprehend what was going on.

Nothing made any sense from up here!

If Bambabele had sent these troops in to mount a counterrevolution, what were they doing on these jungle trails miles from any populated areas, lines of communication, or strategic centers?

"How much fuel have we got left?"

"We'll be all right for a while, sir. I think something's coming through on the radio."

It was the commander of the army detachment from Camp Usomo. His motorized troops had reached the junction with the highlands road. Should they move up toward the Makala Gorge?

Mumungo checked from the window again. He

caught a fleeting glimpse of one of the trucks between the trees. They were driving fast.

"No," he barked. "Stand by at full readiness to move when I give you further orders."

Would these raiders turn south toward the desert again? Or, now they had been spotted, would they try to run for the border? Either way his soldiers could cut them off.

Mumungo ran a pudgy finger around his collar, easing it away from the thick roll of sticky flesh. Whether they planned to retrace their steps or escape into Zaire, he would catch them.

They would be paraded through the streets. And they would know the full force of General Mumungo's fury.

IT COULD NOT BE FAR NOW. They must be close to the bridge. But Yagoda could not tell one stretch of this interminable jungle from another. And that damn plane buzzing overhead like an angry insect only aggravated the tension.

They had made much better time coming back from the mines. The trail was broken in a dozen places by shallow streams, huge root systems that buckled through the surface and matted creepers. But Yagoda had set the pace, pushing his unit as fast as he dared.

Once over that bridge it would not be too far to the railroad yard. Then Scarr could earn his stay of execution. He would have to lead them to the border. But the Russian knew he would have to keep the mercenary separated from the treasure or Scarr might get ideas of his own.

"The bridge is at the bottom of the hill, sir," said Hector, the driver. He eased his foot slightly off the gas, not looking forward to another perilous ride so high above that raging river.

"Don't slow down, man! Keep going. We have to get out of here...."

CROUCHING IN THE DAPPLED SHADOWS, Bolan brushed aside a flowering vine that drooped from the branches above him. His face was set hard, his eyes unflinching as his concentration was focused on the jungle road.

The moment was here.

This was the rendezvous that had been established by those few casual remarks uttered by Jeff Clayton. But this was no game. The rifle in his hand carried thirty rounds of high-velocity ammunition, not yellow marker paint. And the prize wasn't a colored pennant, but a king's ransom in diamonds. A fortune that one man had already murdered for, and that now others would die for.

Here, high above Blood River, it was the killing time.

The first of the trucks appeared, rattled over the roots that had almost tripped Kambolo, and sped down the slope. A thin-faced Cuban with long sideburns was hunched behind the wheel. Bolan recognized the blond passenger, with his flat cheekbones and narrowed eyes, from an earlier sighting at Shoba Well. Boris Yagoda looked remarkably young to be a colonel. He must have proven his dedication to the state.

The Russian looked angry. As the East German vehicle drew level with Bolan's position he could see that Yagoda had his lips tightly compressed and his face was bathed in a film of sweat.

Brendan Scarr was not riding up front with his erstwhile master. Perhaps he had been dealt with and left behind at the mines, dead or alive. No matter. This only confirmed Bolan's suspicions that the payload was in the lead truck. There was no way that the KGB adviser would entrust it to anyone else's care.

The American glanced over to his reluctant subordinate. At least Kambolo seemed to have settled down. The captured Dragunov looked like an unfamiliar object in his hands. All these years the black driver had watched from the edges, standing on the sidelines of life, and now he was caught up in the thick of danger. He cowered in the undergrowth as the Star passed by then rolled to a stop on the bare dirt approach in front of the bridge.

The second of the foreign trucks braked to a halt in the leafy funnel where the road started, just a few feet forward of the position Bolan had calculated. The driver lit a cigarette as he waited for the first vehicle to cross over.

Yagoda climbed out and walked stiffly to the side of the bridge. He automatically looked down at the surging torrent of the Makala before checking the gorge in both directions. All was clear. The far end of the bridge appeared completely deserted. Even the plane had vanished from sight, although it could still be heard in the distance.

Three men had jumped down from the back of the

truck—two Cubans and an Angolan, presumably handpicked as the most trustworthy. From Bolan's vantage point, he could see no one else in there.

The two Cubans trotted forward when Yagoda called them. They did not relish the task to which they had been assigned, but they would do whatever was needed to get themselves out of this accursed country. The Russian commander nodded and they stepped onto the uneven planking of the span, walked out twenty feet and turned. They would be watching that Hector kept the wheels safely aligned.

The Angolan trooper was thankful he had not been ordered to back his way across the bridge giving hand signals for the truck. He slung his rifle on his shoulder and extracted a crumpled cigarette pack from his shirt pocket.

Yagoda gave a quick circling wave to indicate the driver should proceed. Hector let out the clutch slowly, lining up precisely with the bridge entrance. Ten more feet and he would bump out onto that rotted surface.

The Angolan kicked at something on the ground. He bent down and picked up a stainless-steel Zippo, shiny with use, but it could not have been there long.

Bolan felt a chill, realizing that Kambolo must have dropped his lighter. He could almost read the Angolan's thought processes as the man weighed the object in the palm of his hand, glanced quickly around with his eyes widening in alarm, then opened his mouth to call for Yagoda.

Nothing came out but a grunt of pain as Ziemba's arrow ripped through his chest.

The warrior had acted instinctively. Yagoda heard nothing, sensed nothing amiss behind him as he gave his full attention to Hector's maneuvers. But the second driver, seeing his comrade fall, rammed the truck into reverse and gunned the engine.

Bolan half rose, shouting, "Okay, get some!"

## 14

Gary Manning punched the detonator switch. The first staccato rattle of rifle fire was obliterated by the roar of the explosive charge.

A vivid flash seared the forest gloom. The base of the tree trunk was shattered, knocked away from the track; then the tall mahogany toppled over just as the Canadian engineer had so precisely calculated. Tearing itself free from the interlocking branches above and the fettering vines, the heavy tree crashed down onto the trail.

The second truck had reversed so quickly that it slammed into the vehicle behind. In his panic the driver had aligned himself exactly on the spot that Bolan had paced out earlier. The huge tree trunk fell on top of the cab.

The windshield shattered into a thousand fragments as the metal roof caved in. The driver's door buckled open and his senseless body was thrown out onto the track. The other door, already ajar, was sheared from its hinges.

Scarr had reacted instantly—his reflexes honed by a lifetime's practice of self-preservation. Even as the Angolan had clutched convulsively at the feathered shaft protruding from his chest, the Afrikaaner had thrown open his door and rolled clear out of the truck. He scurried into the undergrowth as the falling giant demolished the vehicle he'd been riding in only seconds before.

Bolan traversed to catch Yagoda, but the Russian had already dived for cover. Pistol in hand, he now crouched between the front of the Star and the thick bridge-support post, trying to get a sighting on their unseen attackers.

The two Cubans on the bridge were caught in the open. They were not going back to join in what sounded a hopeless fight. With one startled glance of agreement, the two men turned and ran for the far side.

The RPK's muzzle-flash was a flickering tongue of flame in the distant shrubbery as McCarter raked the center of the span.

One man stumbled forward, blood and mucus hanging in strands from his mouth, as he grappled blindly for the supporting cable, missed, and fell through the gap. Head over heels, spinning awkwardly, his screams drowned out by the raging waters, he plunged into the river.

The other soldier fell to his knees. A second burst twisted him sideways and he collapsed over the edge of the planking. But his foot was trapped in a splintered gap in the bridge flooring, and he hung there in midair, dangling by his ankle, like a slaughtered beast left to bleed.

The dull booming echo of the first explosion had hardly died away when two more sharper bangs rang out. Katz had tossed a pair of grenades into the shouting melee of troopers leaping from the trucks. The frag pattern cut a ghastly swath of destruction through their ranks.

Screaming, scrambling over each other, firing random shots at nothing more substantial than a shadow, Yagoda's unit was broken into an undisciplined mob. Those who tried to seek cover on the right were cut down by short bursts from the Israeli's submachine gun. On the other side, a ruthless enfilade of small-arms fire prevented anyone from escaping into the surrounding jungle.

When Hector Alvarez saw his two friends blown off the bridge, he muttered a prayer and jumped down from the cab. He didn't know which way to turn. The driver had taken only one uncertain pace when another of Ziemba's arrows sliced into its target. It caught Hector in the small of the back. He stood tottering on the cliff edge, then a second shaft slammed between his shoulder blades and knocked him forward. He was dead before his body smashed into the rocks below.

A Cuban, his left leg reduced to crimson tatters by grenade fragments, squirmed for shelter beneath the fallen timber. Kambolo shot him between the eyes then searched for another target. Outnumbered though they still were, the black driver was charged up with a sense of impending victory and the death-spitting strength of the weapon in his hands. He pushed through the bushes, thrilled with the anticipation of another easy score.

Ziemba had dropped from his firing platform in the tree before the intruders could rally themselves and seek out the silent marksman. He linked up with Gary Manning, now working his way back around to Bolan's position.

"The truck," Bolan called out, "get the truck!"

He would take care of Yagoda himself. A full magazine had been expended in pinning down the puppet mercenaries. Bolan reached for a fresh clip as he wriggled through the undergrowth toward the bridgehead.

The Russian was waiting for him. They came upon each other at point-blank range. Yagoda raised his pistol. Bolan swung the empty M-16 like a club and knocked the gun from his hand.

Yagoda lunged out with a slashing karate chop, forcing the American to let go of his rifle. The Russian followed through with a savage kick at Bolan's wounded leg. Then, seeing another white man charging forward, Yagoda turned and raced back toward the front of the truck.

There was nowhere left for him to run but out onto the open bridge itself. Five paces was as far as he got. Bolan seized him in a flying tackle. Yagoda felt a mountain of strength crash into him from behind. His hands flew up to lever away the forearm clamped around his throat. The men from the last of the trucks had managed to regroup. Katz threw another grenade to keep them pinned down and rolled across the track.

Where was Scarr?

Katz was sure he had caught a glimpse of the hated renegade just moments before Gary had blown the tree. There was no sign of Scarr's body in the cab or among those now littering the trail in grotesquely twisted bundles.

The Israeli commando slithered through the bushes, rose to a crouch and circled away from the truck. He wasn't going to let that bastard escape now!

MANNING HAD JUMPED up into the cab of Hector's treasure truck. The engine was still idling. How long could Katz, Kambolo and Ziemba hold off the remnants of Yagoda's company? He had to get the truck across the bridge. He looked up as soon as he had nudged the front wheels onto the first plank. The two leaders were slugging it out hand-to-hand directly in his path!

KATZ PAUSED, cocking his head to catch the slightest sound in the undergrowth that surrounded him. He could hear an Angolan soldier shouting orders, leading the survivors through the trees to his right. But there was someone else. . .someone close by. . . . Katz could sense it with every fiber of his body.

From his hiding place Scarr had seen the Israeli coming. Recognized him. The years had not dimmed his memory of the ex-legionnaire who had commanded the detachment at Shogololo. So that was who had been dogging their trail. Probably to rip off his share of the loot, too, guessed Scarr. It would be doubly enjoyable to disarm the old guy and kill him with his own gun. Scarr ducked back down, hunching into the pit from which he would spring.

Katz whirled at the first shocking gasp of pain.

Scarr was standing less than fifteen feet away. The man's face was contorted in a silent scream of agonized surprise.

The viper had clamped its mouth around his calf. Inch-long fangs were buried in the muscle, injecting a full measure of poison. With a bellow of rage, Scarr tore away the thick sluggish body of the brilliantly camouflaged serpent and staggered forward, grabbing a vine for support.

His face, at first drained of all color, was now mottled with fear. He knew that a serum had to be administered immediately if he were to survive.

Katz fired a quick burst that pulverized the Gabon viper.

"Me," Scarr croaked through lips flecked with pink spittle. "Kill me, too! For God's sake... please!"

Katz began to turn away with a bitter shrug.

It was appropriate that a snake had been the instrument of retribution. But Katz was a man, and it fell to him to show mercy—even to an ancient foe.

He lifted the Uzi and squeezed the trigger. He could have sworn Scarr was almost smiling as he crashed back into the leaves on the forest floor. Katz rammed a fresh magazine into the SMG and hurried back toward the bridge.

From the corner of his eye, Bolan could see the truck drawing closer. Yagoda had thrown him backward and now straddled his body, seeking a strangle hold. Although an inch or two shorter than the

American, Yagoda matched him pound for pound, and none of it was flab.

Bolan, his stiffened right hand held like a spade, rammed into the other man's diaphragm. Yagoda grunted as the breath was forced from his lungs. Bolan unleashed a short left cross to the Russian's face, then bucked hard and threw him off.

Manning could not stop. He heard one of the makeshift planks cracking beneath the rear wheels. It sounded as if the whole groaning bridge was going to give way under him at any moment.

Yagoda recovered his balance and fumbled at the back of his belt. His hand appeared holding a hunting knife. Bolan reached for his own K-bar. The ankle sheath was empty!

The whole structure was trembling with the inexorable advance of the truck.

Bolan suddenly fell flat on his back and let the Star roll right over the top of him. The trick, born out of trust and cunning, worked.

Manning accelerated, driving clean over his comrade-in-arms. The right-side fender caught the Russian with a crunch and knocked him flying. The knife dropped from his numbed fingers and he grabbed for the wire cable. But the fight against the tenacious American had robbed him of that margin of strength he needed to hold on.

With a blood-chilling scream he tumbled into the chasm, never knowing what he was dying for in this hostile land so far from home.

His head smashed on a submerged rock, his blood indistinguishable from the already red-tinted water, and the surging current swept him away. The River of Blood had claimed yet another victim.

The truck past, Bolan sprang up and jumped onto the open tailgate. He took one glimpse inside—the boxes were there! Looking back at the far side, he saw Ziemba staggering across the clearing. The brave archer was clutching at his hip, which had been creased deeply by a Cuban slug. Katz appeared behind him.

"Come on!" shouted Bolan.

Katz looped an arm under the valiant black's shoulder, twisted to fire a last discouraging burst at the road, then together they started hobbling across the bridge.

Ohara ran down to the bridge entrance watching, almost in awe, as Gary Manning deftly maneuvered the lumbering vehicle toward solid ground. Years of experience on backwoods roads and heavy construction projects were now being put to a life-or-death test on the narrow, swaying span.

The Star cleared the bridge.

The lanky Oriental warrior waited for it to pass him, then raced out to give Katz a hand. The two of them helped the staggering Ziemba to safety.

"Run, Kambolo, run!" McCarter had spotted the driver break across the distant clearing.

He dropped the Dragunov as he ran—he'd used up all his ammunition. Half a dozen survivors of Yagoda's unit were crashing through the undergrowth behind him. The Englishman squatted with his finger tense upon the trigger. He could not risk a burst. Kambolo was directly in the line of fire.

The driver was about thirty feet out when the first enemy shot clipped his shoulder. He staggered, his shirt stained red, but continued weaving forward.

"Faster! You can make it!" Encizo stood up and shouted encouragement. Katz and Keio set down their wounded burden and turned to watch Kambolo's hopeless race.

The Porter came in low from the east. The shots and shouts were drowned out by the roar of its engine.

Three Angolans had reached the bridge itself. Their bloodlust was roused to bring down at least one of their opponents.

Kambolo was hit again. This time he fell. Phoenix Force watched as the driver dragged himself to his feet, willing himself onward. He was nearly halfway across.

It looked as if the plane was going to knock both the hunters and their wounded quarry clean off the bridge.

Without warning, Luke Rawson suddenly dived on the detonator and hit the switch. . . .

## 15

The explosion was deafening.

Ohara and Katz, still nearest to the bridge, were knocked flat by the concussive force of the eruption. Rafael Encizo had done his job well. Chunks of old concrete, flailing cables and shattered planking were all hurled into the air through a ball of flame-tinged smoke.

"You crazy bastard!" Encizo's voice was thick with emotion as he whirled and pounced on Rawson.

"The plane...I was trying to get the plane," shouted the surveyor.

But he hadn't succeeded.... The pilot struggled with the controls as the buffeting shock waves tossed the light aircraft about like a kite. He pulled the stick back and climbed high into the sky.

The entire span collapsed as if in slow motion. The wounded Kambolo and his pursuers were hurled into space as the old suspension bridge fell in a snakelike ripple against the far wall of the gorge. As it slammed into the cliff, weighty fragments of reinforcement dragged the broken remains down into the roiling torrent of the Makala River.

McCarter pulled the angry Cuban away from Rawson.

"Bring him over here," ordered Bolan. He turned to Mulanda, who was sitting tensed behind the wheel of the Leopoard Patrol truck. "Get into this one and drive like you've never driven before." He ordered everyone aboard.

McCarter hoisted the machine gun over his shoulder and ran to the newly acquired truck. Encizo gave him a hand to throw in the satchels of explosives.

They were abandoning everything else.

Katz and Ohara lifted Ziemba into the back, then ran forward and clambered up into the cab with the tracker. Bolan almost threw Rawson into the back of the truck with him. He reached down to tug their Cuban colleague up as Mulanda took off down the trail.

The debris had settled but a pall of smoke still hung over the canyon as they plunged down the jungle track and left the River of Blood behind.

ENCIZO DROPPED THE SATCHEL containing the rest of the C-4 next to Manning's gear. He picked up a medical pack and bent over to see what he could do for Ziemba.

McCarter had wiped the blood off the black man's thigh. "Dead lucky you are, mate. Went clean through. Missed the bone. We'll have you strolling down Piccadilly in no time."

Ziemba smiled. The unfamiliar phrases sounded reassuring to him.

Encizo pushed the first-aid kit along the truck

floor toward Bolan. He shook his head. His leg would wait—right now they had to figure out the next move.

He unfolded the map of northeast Kuranda. Finding the tiny uneven circle that represented Lake Baruka, he turned to Rawson. "This is where the plane is, right?"

"Kambolo was a dead man. It was worth trying to get that spotter plane." The surveyor was still trying to justify his actions to anyone who would listen. Nobody was. Bolan's question seemed to snap him out of it. "Yes, that's the place. But you can see we have to take the Omosu road to get there...."

"And by now it'll be crawling with Mumungo's men."

"That pilot's bound to have called them in," agreed Rawson, wiping his mouth with the back of his hand.

"This other place you mentioned, to the east?"

"Mabuti."

"You said there was an airstrip outside Mabuti."

"Just a small one. Kuranda Lumber use it. They keep an old DC-3 out there."

McCarter was listening intently. He glanced at Bolan and nodded emphatically. "If you fellows don't mind a bumpy landing at Kalambasse, I can get us out in a Goony Bird."

"Exactly where is the airfield?"

Rawson traced a dirty fingernail across the map. "See where the railway line disappears through that tunnel before it gets to Mabuti? About a mile to the north, maybe less."

"What's this other line marked here?"

"Overhead power cables. Part of the Makala Hydro System. It was never finished."

"And this is the only road that'll get us there?"

"If it hasn't been washed out," said their guide. "But that's only half the problem. The Omosu-Mabuti road is graded and graveled. We crossed it on the way here, remember? If Mumungo has mobilized his army, they can make much better time than we ever could plowing through that jungle. They'll be able to cut us off before we get near the airfield."

"Maybe so," said Bolan, tapping the threaded line that marked the railroad, "but not if we take a train ride."

ODUKA GAVE the reversing lever a final wipe, then tucked his polishing cloth into the grabrail at the side of the cab. He tapped the cracked glass of the pressure gauge. It would be a few minutes yet before he had enough steam up.

He patted *tembo*'s steel flank fondly as he dropped down beside the track.

The flatcar he had hitched on was half-loaded with bundles of firewood. The caboose at the rear was empty. Oduka did not need to tow it all the way down to Mabuti and back, but he didn't feel it was a proper train without the caboose.

The old railwayman whistled tunelessly as he walked toward his shack behind the engine sheds. He had not yet reached his shack when he heard the truck returning. Oduka started to run for cover, then he stopped. There was not much point—he could not hide *tembo* and the two wagons.

The Communist truck came racing into the yard. Stalks and strands of greenery brushed from the undergrowth bordering the narrow path clung to its front. It drew alongside the tracks and Luke Rawson sprang down from the back.

"Oduka, old friend, we need a ride down to Mabuti."

"That's just where I was going." He sounded somewhat reluctant as he watched the big foreigners helping Ziemba to the ground.

"You hear that plane?" Rawson jerked his thumb toward the screen of trees behind them. "Mumungo's after us!"

Oduka shook his head, wondering what the INGOT surveyor was involved in, but changed it to a nod. "Anyone who is an enemy of Mumungo is a friend of mine."

He even managed a grin for McCarter, whom he recognized as the man who had smashed his window earlier.

The Englishman was still thinking about that DC-3. They were not here to intimidate innocent civilians. He turned to Bolan. "What if someone objects to us borrowing their plane?"

Bolan tapped the nearest of the metal bank boxes. "I'd say we've got enough here to buy that old crate. Now give Rafael a hand and toss this lot in the caboose. Mulanda, hide the truck in the trees over there! It might buy us a few minutes if that plane has to check out the road looking for us."

ODUKA automatically reached for the whistle as they set off. Bolan gently restrained him. "Not this time, my friend."

Manning was working as the fireman on this trip. He gave Bolan a grime-streaked grin as he bent to shovel on more coal. He hadn't had this much fun in ages.

The railroad tracks ran parallel to the road for four or five miles, then veered away to the east. The train picked up speed as it started the long gradual descent to the Mabuti plain. Here the tropical forest was thick and undisturbed. Somewhere ahead, a troop of chimpanzees chattered excitedly, warning each other of the approach of the steaming, straining monster.

Bolan left Manning and Oduka to work the engine. As he climbed back over the coal tender he wondered how long it would be before the plane spotted the thick puffs of smoke that lingered above the trees, marking their escape route.

"How's he doing?" Bolan tipped his head toward Ziemba.

"He'll be fine, bwana." The Mussengamba tracker's smile needed no translation. "He thanks you and the gray-haired one, you do not desert your men."

The two blacks were sitting propped against the mound of firewood, enjoying the sunlight flickering through the trees that lined the tracks. Ohara squatted at the other end of the flatcar, checking how many grenades they had left. Rawson sat close by in sullen silence, staring blankly into the forest.

"You guys okay?" Bolan shouted to Encizo and McCarter, who were perched on top of the caboose.

The Englishman patted the machine gun and gave the Phoenix commander a thumbs-up signal.

Bolan tapped Katz on the arm. "Let's go take a look at what we've got. Have you still got the case?"

The Israeli nodded, picked up the square canvas pack and headed for the rear coach.

The trees were thinning out, the gradient becoming less steep. They could see more of the sky now. But there was still no sign of the plane. Bolan stared down at Rawson and offered him the M-16. "Here, take this, we'll need every gun if there's trouble ahead."

Inside the caboose, Katz opened the bag he was carrying and pulled out a silver-colored case. It was made from an alloy developed for the space program, lightweight but virtually indestructible. He laid it flat on the floor and threw the lid open. Six chamois leather pouches nestled in the thickly padded lining. "Let's hope we've got something to put in them."

Bolan reached for his ankle sheath, remembered it was empty and accepted the heavy combat knife Katz offered him.

He shook the first of the bank boxes. Nothing. It sounded quite empty. He tried another. This time he was rewarded with a metallic rattle. Bolan stuck the blade under the lip of the lid and began to pry it open.

Katz started shaking each of the boxes in turn. If

it sounded promising he shoved it into the pile near Bolan's leg. The others he pushed away for now against the wall of the caboose. "None of them sound as if they have papers inside. . . ."

"Look at this!" Bolan had forced the top off the first container.

He pulled out a dozen gold wafers and a crumbled sack of gold coins. Bolan poured their find into the special carrying case. The next box held seven small nuggets and a loose assortment of minor gems.

"We've reached the open plain," warned Katz, glancing out of the dust-coated window. "I still haven't found. . . ."

"I have," cut in Bolan. He tilted the deposit case so his comrade could see the contents for himself. "Vandergriff's little nest egg!"

There must have been fifty stones in the bottom of that tray. They were roughly shaped and still coated with a cloudy film of dirt. But as Bolan turned the case, pinpricks of light danced in the brilliant depths of the precious gems.

The American poured them into one of the soft leather pouches, silently weighing it in his hand for a moment. He could understand fighting for a cause, sacrificing oneself for a deeply held principle. . . but murdering for a handful of transparent stones. . . . He dropped the pouch into the silver case and started on the next black container.

More diamonds, perhaps forty this time. Plus rings, necklaces and six more thin gold wafers.

Katz shook one of the safe-deposit boxes and lifted

it to his ear. He was sure he heard a faint rustling inside. Was this the real treasure? The one they had come so far and fought so hard for, the papers that Scarr never knew he had stolen?

"Mack, I think. . . ."

There was a sharp rap on the roof as McCarter stamped out a warning. His voice was a tinny echo through the ventilator. "Here comes the army!"

Damn, so Mumungo was taking one last stab at stopping them!

"Yakov, you check it out," said Bolan. "I'll finish here."

Katz hesitated only for a moment, fighting to stifle his curiosity. Mack was right. Colonel Phoenix was the one who had to transfer the rest of the loot to the carrying case, ready to jump off as soon as they got close to the airfield. But the men outside were Katz's primary responsibility. They bore the Phoenix name, but they were his team. "I'll see what's happening."

He had to brace himself against the sway of the coach as Oduka piled on more speed. Katz cocked the Uzi for action and stepped outside.

Bolan reached for the box that Katz had indicated might contain the papers and jammed the knife under the edge of the lid. The lock snapped and Bolan pushed the top open with the blade.

What he saw hit him like a punch in the gut. His breath was expelled in a short, disgusted grunt. So this is what they had risked their lives for. . . .

"Stay right where you are!" Rawson ordered

harshly from the doorway. He slipped inside the caboose.

Bolan looked up to see that his own rifle was now trained right at his chest. But he still reached out to grip the case. "You've come to collect your payoff?"

"I may be leaving Kuranda," the surveyor said, nodding, "but I've got my own way out. And I'm not going empty-handed."

He jerked the barrel of the gun, indicating Bolan should push the silver case toward the door. The American ignored him. "You weren't after that plane back there, were you. You wanted to take out as many of my men as possible, before the time came to turn on me."

"Maybe that's the way it was. Now, gimme the case!"

"What are you going to do with these stones? How do you think you can dispose of them without being caught?"

"I've got my contacts. You can't be in my line of work for twenty years without making some." Rawson risked one quick glance out of the window. "They'll be sold in Antwerp by the end of next week."

"You've already got a buyer?"

"Right from the start, Yank. INGOT said you just needed a guide. But Van Roon called long-distance. He was the one who told me what this deal was all about. He'll take the stones. He specializes in hot property and hard-to-dispose-of merchandise."

"And how the hell did this Van Roon know what we were after?"

Rawson looked momentarily taken aback. Was this Colonel Phoenix trying to put him on? Who else would have set up the deal? "Come on, you should know that! He was already set to buy them, but realized it was to his advantage to deal directly with me."

Bolan paused, his mind pursuing the implications of what Rawson had unwisely admitted. INGOT would have sold off the stones through official channels. They would never have resorted to dealing with a backstreet fence in Amsterdam. That only left one person who could have set this up in advance—someone greedy enough to keep it all to himself.

"So Van Roon pays out a lower purchase price, which you're willing to settle for because you get to keep it all."

"Right. We're both winners. You're the loser, Phoenix, now pass that case over here."

Bolan shook his head. "You'll have to come and get it."

There was more stamping on the ceiling. Katz shouted down, "The plane's coming back, too!"

Bolan glanced up, but Rawson didn't—he was not going to be tricked. "Hurry up! We'll be at the bridge in a few minutes and that's where I'm getting off."

He raised the gun until Bolan found himself staring into the black void of the muzzle. A smile creased the corners of his mouth, as if he were amused at some private joke. "After what you did, you don't think I'd give you a loaded rifle, do you?"

Rawson froze. Hell, it had been Phoenix who pressed the gun in his hands!

That moment's hesitation was all The Executioner needed. He hurled the case upward and deflected the gun. It went off with a deafening roar in the confines of the caboose. But the sound of the M-16 firing was lost amid the defiant fusillade unleashed from the roof above and out on the flatcar. Phoenix Force had two trucks, a jeep, and three armored cars to contend with. The road ran right beside the railway track and Mumungo's men had nearly caught up with the train.

The bullet tore a hole in the wall, but Rawson still had a grip on the rifle. He brought the butt up hard and clipped Bolan on the side of the head, then parried the knife curving it from the left.

Bolan grabbed the barrel, twisting the rifle away, but Rawson now had hold of his wrist. The two men smashed each other into the wooden walls of the caboose, and they both sought the final decisive advantage.

Angered at his own stupidity for talking too long; frustrated by years of unrewarding service; fearful that his last chance to make good was slipping from his grasp, Rawson fought like a man possessed. He was as tough a foe as the Executioner had ever faced in personal combat.

The surveyor kneed him in the groin and dragged his heel down sharply on the wounded leg. The M-16 was pressing lengthwise across Bolan's throat as

Rawson hammered the back of his head against the hard planking.

One of the windows shattered. A bullet from outside splintered into the ceiling. The sound of more shots and engines racing to keep abreast of the train accompanied the private duel within.

Rawson was leather tough and utterly without scruples. He may have made a mistake in letting the American make him talk, but he was not about to fool himself again. He knew this fight was to the finish. Only one of them would be getting off this train.

For one second, Bolan let go of the rifle. Rawson sensed he had the upper hand and tried to flatten the other man's windpipe. He did not see Bolan's hands stiffening into axheads of hardened flesh before both slashed inward at Rawson's trunk. The surveyor's breath was suddenly knocked out of him. Bolan rammed a kneecap in Rawson's groin. He staggered back to the center of the car, doubling over as fiery needles of unbearable pain stabbed through his insides.

The Executioner tangled his fingers in the man's hair, dragging him forward, keeping him facedown as the other iron fist rearranged his features.

Blood was spurting from his nose and a corner of his mouth as Bolan spun him around and sent him crashing to the floor.

But the agony was not finished. His body flipped over to slam into the floorboards; Bolan was still holding his arm. Rawson felt the tendons separate, the muscles tearing as the grim-faced warrior methodically broke the South African's arm at the shoulder.

The pain was still building to a crescendo when he lost consciousness.

BOLAN LEAPED ACROSS THE GAP onto the flatcar. A truckload of black soldiers was almost level with them. Ohara was bent low behind a makeshift barricade of Oduka's firewood. He waited for the precise moment and threw two grenades, then two more.

One landed in the back of the speeding vehicle. Another blew the left front wheel clean off the axle. The truck slewed sideways, then rolled over to crush the few troopers who had not been wounded by the first explosion.

McCarter was concentrating his machine-gun fire on an armored car, which swerved to avoid the wreckage of the truck.

One man, miraculously not hurt, had been thrown clear. He staggered to his feet, stumbling in confusion—right in the path of the armored car. It went straight over him. This time he stayed down.

"The jeep! Get that jeep!" Katz was rallying the men to concentrate their firepower on the machine that was racing away on their flank, trying to draw ahead of the train.

Clutching the silver case, Bolan worked his way forward.

"Can you give us more speed?"

Oduka shook his head. *Tembo* could go no faster.

Bolan touched Manning on the shoulder. "There's

a bridge up ahead where the road crosses the rails. If they get there first they'll blow it down and block the rails, but if we can beat them, can you rig the caboose?"

"Sure. Let's go!"

Crouchwalking, they reached the flatcar.

"Give me two minutes," yelled the engineer.

"You've got about ninety seconds," Bolan told him, checking the curving track ahead and seeing the bridge in the distance. "Rafael! Yakov! All of you, get back down here!"

Mulanda and Keio provided a steady stream of covering fire as the other three members of Phoenix Force clambered down from the roof.

Bolan threw a couple of grenades, straddling the road with smoking gouts of dirt and grit. The second armored car rocked high onto two wheels, then crashed back down, but too late for the driver to regain control before it smashed into a power pylon at the side of the road.

The spotter plane was approaching low and fast.

Oduka was glancing back from the side window to catch Bolan's signal when he had to brake. It would only be for a moment, just long enough to ease the tension on the coupling that held the caboose.

Encizo was ready to unhitch the rear coach.

Leaping over the crouching figure of the Cuban, Manning landed on the flatcar. "The fuse is lit!"

Bolan signaled the driver.

The bridge was just ahead now. The men had piled out of the jeep. Two of them pointed their rifles at the approaching train; the others were unloading the explosives.

The young officer was still feverishly trying to connect the detonator wires when *tembo* flashed past beneath them.

Encizo had already snapped open the coupling.

They began to pull away from the caboose.

Manning grabbed Bolan's attention. "You know Rawson was lying inside there?"

"Yeah," Bolan said, nodding, "he said that's where he wanted to get off."

The last armored car reached the bridge at the same moment the caboose exploded.

The center of the span peeled upward, huge slabs of pavement being blown sky high, while the tattered ends of the bridge collapsed into the smoking gap.

MUMUNGO SCREAMED an oath and punched the pilot in the shoulder. Both men were looking down at the large dust-filled crater stretching between the buckled rails when the Pilatus Porter flew straight into the high-voltage wires of the uncompleted hydro project.

The plane blew apart on impact, orange red flashes within a rumbling oil-black smokeball. Phoenix Force gave Mumungo a last rousing cheer. No one would follow them to the airfield.

FIVE SMALL STONES bought the Goony Bird.

Matuka, who sold it to them, did not own the plane. He did not even know what it was worth. He was just the security guard.

They were airborne within ten minutes. McCarter could not resist a brief victory waggle as they circled once over the shattered ruins of the bridge.

Through the address system he kept them amused all the way back to Kalambasse.

The Englishman was in the middle of a long-winded and very off-color story about an archbishop and a young actress when he pancaked across the dark surface of the lake.

Hohenadel and Sorbara were standing by for them.

## 16

The snow lay thick and fresh. It had only stopped snowing at 4:00 P.M. the previous day—two hours before Bolan and Katz flew into Toronto.

In the street outside the hotel it was piling into grimy slush. But out here beyond the city it was still a soft white blanket.

"Pontiac, blue. Two men," reported Katz, as he spotted the surveillance car.

They said nothing else as they approached the sprawling mock-Tudor mansion. The silver case lay cushioned on the back seat.

Bolan could see no sign of the horses. The stables looked shut up. But a Ferrari Berlinetta Boxer sat parked in the graveled driveway. They pulled to a halt in front of the stately house.

The two men stood in front of the heavy wooden door, and exchanged one resolute glance; then Bolan punched the bell.

Malakesi opened the door. "Do come in, Colonel Phoenix."

The distinguished aide led them through to the same lounge where Bolan had first heard of Scarr's treasure and the River of Blood.

Malakesi offered the visitors some refreshment.

Bolan asked for a Scotch. Katzenelenbogen took a vodka and tonic. The ex-justice minister smiled as he handed them their drinks. "We heard General Mumungo was killed in an unfortunate air accident while he was inspecting a new hydro project...."

Malakesi's words were cut off by the sound of a door being shut. Bambabele entered the room. He wore a gold turtleneck sweater, light tweed jacket and a very business-like expression.

"We were expecting you to call us first, Colonel."

Bolan gave an indifferent shrug. "But you were expecting us."

Bambabele averted his eyes and caught sight of the metal case by the side of Bolan's chair. For the first time he smiled. "You found them!"

"No," Bolan corrected him, "we had to take them."

"Of course, of course. But the diamonds, they were there?"

"Aren't you interested in the papers?"

It was Malakesi who nodded, not the ex-prime minister. "Well, have you retrieved the documents?"

Bolan reached into his coat pocket. His hand re-emerged in a closed fist. He looked at the two politicians and opened his hand. A cloud of gray dust, together with some larger scraps, fluttered onto the carpet.

"Termites! They'll eat anything and everything, including all your precious papers." Bolan never took his eyes off Bambabele. "But you probably knew that even before we set off. You never were interested in the papers, were you?"

The former Kuranda leader turned away disdainfully, seeming to dismiss such a suggestion. When he suddenly turned back, he was holding a Mauser semiautomatic.

"You used us to steal the diamonds," came Bolan's cold accusation. He ignored the pistol pointed at him. "You used INGOT, Jeff Clayton, some good people inside your own country. . . . You didn't care who got hurt as long as you got hold of the diamonds."

"Why should I share Kuranda's wealth with an international conglomerate?"

"You don't intend to share it with anyone!" scoffed Bolan. "You've already arranged to sell these stones in Antwerp. To one Van Roon, I believe. You should have picked a more trustworthy fence."

Bambabele remained quite stony faced, betraying no curiosity as to how the American had discovered these arrangements. It was Malakesi who shook his head sadly, not wanting to believe the ugly charges. But the 9mm pistol in Bambabele's hand was eloquent confirmation.

"I won't let you!" Malakesi quivered with fury at being betrayed. He took a step forward. "You cannot steal. . . ."

Bambabele fired only once. It hit Malakesi in the chest. Dead center.

The ex-justice minister was thrown against the wall. His legs buckled slowly and his body left a vivid, sticky smear down the paintwork as he collapsed to the floor.

Bambabele was no amateur. Not like Luke Rawson. He would waste no more time talking than he had to. "Move back, both of you! Keep your hands higher."

"You just screwed your chances for political asylum," said Bolan.

"The diamonds will buy me refuge in any of a dozen countries," replied Bambabele confidently, picking up the lightweight container. "You're the ones in trouble. Two men, easily proved to be mercenaries, shot dead in a gun battle with an African diplomat, himself once a guerrilla."

"And you?"

"Oh, I shall have fled in fear of my life, Colonel Phoenix. It will be a long time before I...."

Katz fired the built-in .22 just as Bambabele hefted the case in front of him. The hollowpoint slug smashed a large dent in the front cover and almost knocked Bambabele off balance.

The black leader snapped off another shot, just missing Katz, turned and fled.

The Israeli recovered his poise and was about to charge after him.

"No." Bolan stopped his friend. There was a look of bitter disappointment in his eyes. He had not wanted it to end this way. "Let him go."

They turned to the window and saw the Ferrari speeding away around the curve of the front drive.

BAMBABELE PASSED the Pontiac and drove on over the hill. His other car, a nondescript Buick with everything he needed already packed, was stashed at an abandoned farm about ten miles farther on.

But curiosity gnawed at him and—a growing suspicion that Colonel John Phoenix might have tried a last-minute double-cross.

He pulled off to the side of the road and checked the mirror. The Pontiac had not followed him. They were used to his comings and goings, he'd made sure of that. They would stay back there to log his return. Well, they were in for a long, cold wait.

He turned to the case lying on the passenger seat. Bambabele's delicate hands were trembling with excitement as he undid the latches.

Holding his breath, he jerked the lid open.

It had worked!

Six bulging pouches lay cocooned in the soft black lining.

And a thread dangled from the left-hand side of the lid.

It had just pulled the pin from the grenade that Bolan had taped securely to the inside wall of the case.

Bambabele realized he had only a few seconds left to live. Desperately he reached out to slam the lid shut.

But Bolan had outwitted him even on the final move.

It was short fused.

Bambabele saw only a pinprick of light, glowing white-hot. And the sound. Like the roar of a. . . .

Thousands of tiny steel balls cut Bambabele to shreds before the blood-drenched windows exploded outward. Two seconds later the gas tank erupted.

BACK AT THE MANSION Bolan picked up his Scotch and turned to Katz. "Here's to the people of Kuranda...whoever their new leader might be!"

# Don Pendleton on
# MACK BOLAN

If the well-researched quality of *Ambush on Blood River* is *very* familiar to seasoned Bolan fans, it's because of Alan Bomack. Alan's work appeared previously in *The Invisible Assassins* (Executioner #53), a highly topical story set in Japan, and I can tell you he's a guy who knows what he's writing about.

Bomack's an ex-journalist who's lived in Africa and the terrorist-plagued Middle East. He's as familiar with Paris and London as you and I are with Las Vegas, San Diego or Indianapolis! Those of you who've read the saga about *ninjas* and bacteriological warfare will appreciate the degree to which his stories are torn from today's headlines.

In *Ambush*, Alan is back at his gutsy best with a story about the tragic character of Africa, where man wrestles raw nature in a timeless hellground. I know you'll get a lot out of his vision of Africa, because Alan Bomack has captured the hard essence of The Executioner and sees the dark continent through Mack's own eyes.

Also, he realizes Mack's life is an exhilarating adventure that we all share, and to which we can all contribute some meaningful dimension. Alan understands that deep down in our hearts, we dig the guy because we *are* the guy.

Stay hard.

*Don Pendleton*

# MACK BOLAN

**THE EXECUTIONER 59**

## appears again in
## Crude Kill

A master assassin had commandeered the largest oil tanker in the world. The crazed savage threatened to blow up the ship and turn the Mediterranean into a giant oil slick.

Mack Bolan boards the tanker as a one-man assault squad. He strikes like lightning again and again until it comes down to just two men: Bolan against the assassin.

Deep in the steel bowels of the ship, Bolan tracks his prey. Suddenly he hears the sound of a grenade spoon popping off. His foot has brushed against it in the darkness. Now the little deathmaker is activated. Bolan will be dead in 4.4 seconds....

# HE'S EXPLOSIVE.
# HE'S UNSTOPPABLE.
# HE'S MACK BOLAN!

He learned his deadly skills in Vietnam...then put them to use by destroying the Mafia in a blazing one-man war. Now **Mack Bolan** is back to battle new threats to freedom, the enemies of justice and democracy—and he's recruited some high-powered combat teams to help. **Able Team**—Bolan's famous Death Squad, now reborn to tackle urban savagery too vicious for regular law enforcement. And **Phoenix Force**—five extraordinary warriors handpicked by Bolan to fight the dirtiest of anti-terrorist wars around the world.

Fight alongside these three courageous forces for freedom in all-new, pulse-pounding action-adventure novels! Travel to the jungles of South America, the scorching sands of the Sahara and the desolate mountains of Turkey. And feel the pressure and excitement building page after page, with nonstop action that keeps you enthralled until the explosive conclusion! Yes, Mack Bolan and his combat teams are living large...and they'll fight against all odds to protect our way of life!

**Now you can have all the new Executioner novels delivered right to your home!**

You won't want to miss a single one of these exciting new action-adventures. And you don't have to! Just fill out and mail the coupon following and we'll enter your name in the Executioner home subscription plan. You'll then receive four brand-new action-packed books in the Executioner series every other month, delivered right to your home! You'll get two **Mack Bolan** novels, one **Able Team** and one **Phoenix Force.** No need to worry about sellouts at the bookstore...you'll receive the latest books by mail as soon as they come off the presses. That's four enthralling action novels every other month, featuring all three of the exciting series included in The Executioner library. Mail the card today to start your adventure.

**FREE! Mack Bolan bumper sticker.**

When we receive your card we'll send your four explosive Executioner novels and, absolutely FREE, a Mack Bolan "Live Large" bumper sticker! This large, colorful bumper sticker will look great on your car, your bulletin board, or anywhere else you want people to know that you like to "Live Large." And you are under no obligation to buy anything—because your first four books come on a 10-day free trial! If you're not thrilled with these four exciting books, just return them to us and you'll owe nothing. The bumper sticker is yours to keep, FREE!

Don't miss a single one of these thrilling novels...mail the card now, while you're thinking about it. And get the Mack Bolan bumper sticker FREE!

# BOLAN FIGHTS AGAINST ALL ODDS TO DEFEND FREEDOM!

## Mail this coupon today!